Court Fielding stared out the library window.

But he did not see the sweeping expanse of lawn or the swimming pool or tennis court beyond, mellowed by twilight. He saw the woman, her flashing dark eyes, her expressive face framed by the rolled brim of her lilac-flowered straw hat, wisps of dark ringlets escaping from her neat French knot. He saw her tall lithe body in a modest silk shirtwaist. A woman who once would have attracted him, who would have found him attractive. Before. . . But now such a woman was only a cruel reminder of what was. What might have been.

No, he did not want the boy here, disrupting the solitude and quiet of his life. But even more he could not bear the presence of the woman.

RACHEL DRUTEN is a native Californian. She is an artist as well as an author, wife, mother, and grandmother. Much of her time is devoted to overseeing a nonprofit, on-site, after-school program in the arts for disadvantaged children, K through 5.

Books by Rachel Druten

HEARTSONG PRESENTS
HP312—Out of the Darkness (with Dianna Crawford)
HP363—Rebellious Heart
HP508—The Dark Side of the Sun

The Healing Heart

Rachel Druten

Heartsong Presents

To my mother, Noel Bryant, and my friend, Barbara Hillman, who inspire with an example of how faith and an indomitable spirit can transcend the body's limitations.

I am grateful to Dianna Crawford, Sheila Herron, and of course, my husband, Charles, and his red pencil; my patient, tenacious editor at Barbour, Debbie Cole, who doesn't let me get by with a thing; and my family and friends who continue to support and encourage me.

A note from the Author:
I love to hear from my readers! You may correspond with me by writing:

> **Rachel Druten**
> **Author Relations**
> **PO Box 719**
> **Uhrichsville, OH 44683**

ISBN 1-58660-862-2

THE HEALING HEART

All Scripture quotations are taken from the King James Version of the Bible.

All of the characters and events in this book are fictitious. Any resemblance to actual persons, living or dead, or to actual events is purely coincidental.

PRINTED IN THE U.S.A.

one

June, 1947

"Are you sure this is the right address?"

"It's the address you gave me, Lady. Seven Amherst Point." The cabbie slowed as he drove between the columns that flanked the entrance to the estate.

Rebecca glanced again at the letter clutched in her hand—Daisy's letter with the directions. *Yes. Seven Amherst Point. That's right.*

Jacaranda trees lined the winding drive, carpeting their path with fallen purple blooms that popped and crunched beneath the cab's wheels. Through the lace of branches Rebecca glimpsed the gabled stone mansion, perched at the crest of the sloping hill like a bird of prey preparing to take flight.

She'd had no idea it was so grand.

A lump of concern clogged her throat, and she was suddenly aware of her racing heart.

"Mommy, are we almost there?"

She looked down at her four-year-old son beside her. His eyes glittered with anticipation and trust. "Yes, Davy, I think we are." For his sake she must remain calm.

The cab stopped with a jolt.

Even before Rebecca and Davy disembarked, the driver had leaped from the vehicle and pulled their three pieces of modest luggage from the trunk. He dropped them at the bottom of the broad stone steps leading up to the entry. "That'll be three dollars."

Rebecca opened her purse and began counting out the bills.

The mansion's double doors suddenly flew open, and a large, buxom woman, in a flowered dress and pale gray sweater, hurried out waving her gloved hands. "Wait!" she called.

She disappeared for an instant then reappeared, holding a small suitcase in one hand, a large black handbag in the other. A tiny rose-covered hat teetered on her tightly permed gray hair as she scurried down the steps. "This'll save me having to call another taxi," she said, yanking open the cab door and tossing in her luggage. She turned back to Rebecca. "Mrs. Spaneas?"

Rebecca nodded.

"I'm Neda Roberts, the Fieldings' cook. Sorry to leave you in the lurch this way, but my daughter just delivered. For the fourth time. I'll be helping her out for the next month or so."

Rebecca laid the money in the driver's hand. "I'm sure Daisy and I can—"

"Oh, Miss Daisy won't be here either. She hightailed it east a week ago. Too late to let you know. A wedding. Some friend from college. There's a letter for you on the table in the entry. I'm sure it'll explain everything." For the first time the woman's gaze dropped to Davy.

"My son," Rebecca said, squeezing his hand.

The woman observed him with lifted brows. "This should be interesting. I wish I were a fly on the wall."

"Hey, Lady! The meter's running!" the cabbie yelled.

"Sorry—gotta go." Neda Roberts jumped into the cab. "Good luck." She slammed the car door shut and rolled down the window. "You're gonna need it."

Rebecca watched the cab do a one-eighty and swing back down the drive. "I wonder what she meant by that." Taking a deep breath, she looked down at her son. "Well, Mr. Davy," she said softly, "what do you think?"

"It's big," Davy said, staring up at the imposing structure.

"That it is."

Backlit by the late afternoon sun, the mansion loomed above them, even larger and more formidable than it had seemed from a distance.

"It's too big. I don't think I want to live here." Davy's voice quavered.

"There could be all sorts of happy surprises inside," Rebecca said with forced cheerfulness. "Besides, I think George would be very disappointed after sailing all the way from the Philippines if we didn't at least take a peek. Isn't that right, George?" She addressed the stuffed sock monkey clutched in the child's hand. The doll's fat red lips returned its perpetual smile.

"See. I was right," she said. "Are you strong enough to carry your toys, Davy?"

"I'm very strong." He picked up the small, bulging duffle bag and followed Rebecca as she struggled up the steps, a suitcase in either hand.

They crossed the shaded veranda and put their luggage down in front of the immense carved doors. The doors had been left slightly ajar; but rather than enter, Rebecca knocked tentatively.

There was no answer.

"Maybe you better ring the bell," Davy suggested.

"Good idea."

They could hear chimes and then an impatient male voice. "Come in."

Lifting their luggage again, they stepped into the almost chilling coolness of the large oval entry.

"Oh," Davy whispered.

Glittering in the beam of a skylight two stories above, a chandelier hung down into the center of the room. Its cut-crystal prisms cast an infinite array of tiny rainbows over the paneled walls and hardwood floor. Beyond the sweeping staircase on their left, Rebecca could see down a short hall to a solarium and through an arch on their right, the living room with its great stone fireplace, crown moldings, and oriental rugs. Crimson plush, overstuffed furniture was arranged in groupings about a room that seemed only slightly smaller than the whole plantation cottage in which she had been raised.

But even though the room was breathtakingly lovely, it—the whole mansion in fact—had the musty odor of a home that had been closed for a season and a strangely dreary aspect, as if the occupants were in mourning.

The drapes were closed. She saw few plants in the solarium, no flowers in the antique vase on the carved cherry-wood table in the entry—only an envelope, affixed with her name.

She picked it up.

"Come into the library," the same male voice commanded, as impatient as before.

Davy pressed closer. "I don't like this place," he whispered. "He sounds like an ogre."

Rebecca couldn't have agreed more. With each moment her own heart was sinking. This was not at all the greeting she'd expected. Her younger sister, Imogene, had given such glowing reports of her happy-go-lucky school chum Daisy and especially of Daisy's handsome brother, Court.

Now here she and Davy were, abandoned by the carefree Daisy, and if his voice was any indication, thrust into the lair of a most unpleasant—well, if he wasn't an ogre, he certainly sounded like one.

"Come through the living room," the disembodied voice ordered.

"Thank you very much," Rebecca muttered to herself and grabbed Davy's hand. Irritation was fast replacing anxiety.

She knocked on the library door.

"It's open."

Rebecca and Davy stood in the entrance of the book-lined library. This room, too, was dim, lit only by a narrow rectangle of light pushing between the partially parted drapes. In front of it, the silhouette of a figure in a wheelchair. Presumably Courtney Fielding III.

His back was to them, and he made no sign that he was aware of their presence.

Rebecca cleared her throat. "Mr. Fielding?"

"Ah, at last, my baby-sitter has arrived."

"You're not a baby," Davy piped before Rebecca could stop him.

Courtney Fielding wheeled around. He stared at Davy, then at Rebecca, then back at Davy. A menacing scowl marred his otherwise handsome features. "What is *he* doing here?"

"He's my son." Rebecca laid a protective hand on Davy's shoulder. "Didn't Daisy tell you?"

"No! She did not." Courtney Fielding reached over and snapped on the lamp sitting on the desk beside him. Its soft glow lit the lower reaches of the book-lined library and the maroon leather furniture. For a long moment he studied Rebecca, then Davy.

Davy stared back. "I don't think George likes you very much," he murmured, holding up his monkey doll, as he pressed closer against Rebecca.

"That's no way to talk, Davy." Rebecca gave his shoulder a warning squeeze.

The man's lips lifted in a lean smile. "As a matter of fact, I don't much care for monkeys either." His cool blue eyes held a glint of amusement, but when he turned his gaze on Rebecca his face was without expression. "I'm sorry, Mrs. Spaneas. I'm afraid this isn't going to work out. This is not a house for children. You can sleep here tonight. Tomorrow I'll have someone find you and your boy another place to stay."

two

At first Rebecca did not believe what she'd just heard. "Surely you're not saying—"

"Look around you, Mrs. Spaneas. It wouldn't be fair to the boy to live in a place like this. And, as you can see, I'm in no position to deal with him."

Her throat constricted. "Davy is very obedient. He wouldn't—"

Courtney Fielding shook his head. "I'm sorry. It's just not possible for you to stay here."

"Doesn't he want us?" Davy's expression was as perplexed as it was trusting.

A shiver of despair ran through Rebecca. She looked down at the man in the wheelchair and could muster little pity. So smug in the midst of his abundance. Obviously never a moment's concern for whether he would have food on his table or a roof over his head—to say nothing of caring for a child. Courtney Fielding hadn't just lost the use of his legs; he'd lost his heart.

Reckless words rushed from her. "Are you telling me, Mr. Fielding, that I came all the way from the Philippines to hear this? That I spent five weeks sailing across the Pacific Ocean with my four-year-old son on a chance?" Anger roiled within her. "When your sister, Daisy, hired me—begged me, to be more accurate—to be your housekeeper, she knew exactly what she was getting. She knew Davy was part of the package. She paid both our passages. Does that sound as if we came on some whim?"

"Please, Mrs. Spaneas, calm down."

"Calm down?" Rebecca's voice cracked.

"The operative word here, Mrs. Spaneas, is Daisy." The man's tone was condescending. "Your dealings were with Daisy, not with me. She hired you; I didn't. I never would have done so, knowing your"—he glanced at Davy—"encumbrance."

"Encumbrance? I hardly think of my child as an encumbrance, Mr. Fielding."

"I can understand that, Mrs. Spaneas. But for this position I'm afraid that's just what he is."

"What's a cumbrance, Mommy?"

"It doesn't matter, Darling. It has nothing to do with you," Rebecca said sharply, blinking back tears.

Davy took his mother's hand and looked sternly at the man in front of him. "You make my mommy sad. My daddy doesn't like you, too."

"Davy—"

"Your daddy?" Courtney Fielding frowned and glanced at Rebecca. "I thought—"

"Daddy's in heaven," Davy said. "An' he watches over me and Mommy, an' he looks at you, too. He knows you're mean."

"Davy!" Horrified, Rebecca shushed him—even though he *was* speaking the truth.

"Don't shush the boy." A ghost of a smile played across the man's lips. "He's absolutely right. I am mean. So why on earth, Mrs. Spaneas, would you want to work for me?"

"It's not a matter of *want*, Mr. Fielding. It's a matter of *need*. I need to work. I am the sole support of my child and myself." She glanced around the elegantly appointed room. "I do not have an inheritance to depend on."

She grabbed Davy's hand. Rising to her full five-feet eight inches, she glared down at the man in the wheelchair. "I'm a good worker, and I'm loyal. Your loss, Mr. Fielding, will be someone else's gain." She turned on her heel and, dragging Davy along, strode toward the door.

"I'm not going to throw you out into the street, Mrs. Spaneas. I'm not totally heartless."

"You could have fooled me," Rebecca muttered, pausing in the entrance.

"What was that?"

"Nothing."

"I'm expecting a call from Daisy tonight. She and I will discuss what to do with you."

As if she and Davy were refuse to be taken to the dump.

He wheeled his chair toward her across the oriental rug. "In the meantime you can stay in the housekeeper's quarters."

"Mommy"—Davy was shifting from foot to foot—"I need to tell you something." He tugged on her sleeve until she bent close and he could whisper in her ear.

Rebecca straightened. "Do you have a powder room nearby, Mr. Fielding?"

"It's there." He nodded toward a door down the hall. "Opposite the elevator."

"A elevator." For a moment Davy forgot his purpose. "You got a elevator?"

"Yes. I find it convenient at bedtime."

"It's not a toy, Davy," Rebecca said sternly, breaking in before Davy had a chance to delve further. Taking his hand, she ignored the lifted brow and eyes that seemed to say, *I told you this house was unsuitable for a child.*

❧

Courtney Fielding was waiting by the elevator when Rebecca and Davy emerged from the powder room.

"I almost couldn't hold it," Davy confided.

"I don't think Mr. Fielding cares, Dear," Rebecca murmured.

"On the contrary, I'm relieved to know he's housebroken. Where's your luggage?"

The man was impossible. "In the entry."

"There are back stairs next to the kitchen, but it'll be easier to take your things up in the elevator."

When they returned, the elevator was open, his wheelchair blocking the door. Davy carried his small duffel bag in one hand and George in the other, the monkey's stuffed-sock feet dusting the polished oak floor. Rebecca struggled behind with the two suitcases.

"I'll take one of those," Courtney Fielding reached for the heaviest, hefting it easily onto his lap.

The metal gates of the elevator clanged shut. The door closed.

"Can you count?" he asked Davy.

Davy nodded. "I'm not a baby."

"Well, then push button two."

With a shiver and a clank the elevator began to rise slowly. It lurched to a stop on the second floor. The doors slid open and then the gates. Rebecca and Davy followed their host into a broad hall with walls of burnished mahogany and a plush ivory carpet that silenced their steps. At the end, a length of the house away, a door opened into a short, narrow hallway. Rebecca could see into a cheery-looking sewing room on their right and the back stairs at the far end.

Courtney Fielding opened the door opposite.

The housekeeper's suite was in the farthest corner of the manor, facing the front. The blinds were closed, and the tiny sitting room was dim and as sparse and humbly furnished as the rest of the mansion was grand.

He reached up and turned on the light.

The bald bulb in the center spread a harsh yellow glow over the worn tweed couch and mismatched armchair and the kidney-bean-shaped coffee table between. A table with a laminated top and two chairs sat beneath the window. On the wall beside the door leading into the bedroom there was only the shadow of an absent picture. The best that could be said was the room was clean.

"You'll find sheets and towels in the sewing room," he said, putting Rebecca's suitcase beside the couch and backing his wheelchair out into the hall. "Help yourself to anything in the kitchen."

The door between the main part of the house and the servants' quarters slammed shut behind him.

☙

Court Fielding stared out the library window. But he did not see the sweeping expanse of lawn or the swimming pool or tennis court beyond, mellowed by twilight. He saw the woman, her flashing dark eyes, her expressive face framed by the rolled brim of her lilac-flowered straw hat, wisps of dark ringlets escaping from her neat French knot. He saw her tall lithe body in a modest silk shirtwaist. A woman who once would have attracted him, who would have found him attractive. Before. . . But now such a woman was only a cruel reminder of what was. What might have been.

No, he did not want the boy here, disrupting the solitude and quiet of his life. But even more he could not bear the presence of the woman.

three

The dreary room echoed Rebecca's misery. She dropped onto the edge of the couch and buried her face in her hands. The tears came. She had no will left to stop them.

She had always felt God's presence and protection. Even through those torturous years of the Japanese occupation. Even on that terrible day when she'd learned that her beloved husband, David—her knight in shining armor, her hero— had been tortured and murdered, God was there to comfort and sustain her. Through it all, her faith had remained stead-fast. Unlike her sister, Imogene, who had struggled, Rebecca had never for more than a moment questioned God's power or His love.

Her faith was what had given her the courage to come to America and start a new life. Her hopes had been too high to be so recklessly, ruthlessly dashed.

She pulled off her hat and threw it carelessly onto the couch beside her and, taking deep breaths, wiped away the telltale signs of weakness. But she'd had such dreams for Davy's and her future. And now, before even one night had passed. . . .

Her family a continent away, no friends to turn to. All she had were the few dollars in her purse, some shabby belongings in the suitcase—she gave it a small kick—and her memories.

For the first time in her life she wondered if God had forgotten her.

She squeezed her eyes shut against another spate of tears. Still, some escaped leaving dark splotches on her pale dress.

"Oh, dear God, help me. I am so alone."

Only when she felt the touch of a small hand on hers did she realize she had said the words aloud and that her young son stood staring up at her.

"You're not alone, Mommy. I'm here."

She drew Davy close, appalled at her own self-indulgent suffering. Shame and guilt, the curses of motherhood, fell over her. "I'm so sorry, Davy." She kissed his cheeks. "As long as you and Mommy stay together, neither of us will ever be alone."

"And Daddy's with us, Mommy. Remember—he's always watching over us."

"He certainly is." She smoothed the dark curls back from her child's troubled brow. As always, she was struck by how much he resembled his father.

"And Jesus is," Davy murmured, resting his head against her breast.

She gave a small, shuddering sigh. "And Jesus."

❧

Wearily, Rebecca leaned her head against the closed library door and knocked gently.

"Yes?"

"I'm making dinner for Davy and me, Mr. Fielding. May I make yours as well?"

"Don't bother. I can take care of myself."

"It's no bother. Shall I bring it to the library?"

"I may be a cripple, Mrs. Spaneas, but I'm not infirm. I take my meals in the dining room."

"Very well." Rebecca turned and was a stride away when she heard his muffled voice again. "Was there something else?" she asked.

"Thank you," he repeated.

"My pleasure." She wondered if he sensed her sarcasm.

Rebecca flicked on the kitchen light, and her breath

caught. It rivaled the library in size and was better equipped than most restaurant kitchens with its two refrigerators and an eight-burner range with double ovens. Cooking pots and pans hung from hooks above the stove, and every kind of appliance imaginable was visible along the wood counters.

Her baker's heart leaped at the sight of the marble slab for making pastries.

But even though it was large, the kitchen had a homey, cheerful aspect with the trestle table, nicked and scratched with years of use, that occupied the center of the waxed pine floor.

"The kitchen is—is—" Davy spread his arms wide.

"Gigantic," Rebecca offered. Oh, what wonders she could have concocted here had she been given the chance.

"It makes me hungry," Davy said.

"Me, too." She lifted him onto one of the four kitchen chairs and pushed him up to the table. "Let's see what I can find to tide you over."

The first refrigerator held only a few sodas, but Neda Roberts, the cook, had left the second well stocked: a roast and a frying chicken in the meat compartment, fresh vegetables, a bowl of apples, two chicken pies and a meatloaf ready to bake, a bottle of milk and one of orange juice, butter and eggs.

Rebecca cut some carrot and celery sticks for Davy. She hulled fresh peas and sliced tomatoes which she bathed in a vinaigrette dressing and returned to the refrigerator to marinate.

"I think we need some comfort food," she said when she discovered some stale white bread in the back of the bread-box. Before long the scent of cinnamon and nutmeg in a rich bread pudding mingled with that of the roasting meat and baking potatoes.

"I don't want to eat with the mean man," Davy said.

"And you don't have to. You and I are going to eat right here on this beautiful table in the kitchen. Mr. Fielding eats in the dining room."

Davy wriggled out of the chair. "Can I help set the table?"

Between the kitchen and dining room the butler's pantry shelves were filled with fine china, crystal and linens from which Rebecca made her choice. She pushed open the swinging door into the dining room.

"Wow!" Davy cried. "It has a fireplace."

A grand Sheraton mahogany table with ten matching chairs ran down the center of the oak-paneled room. In the middle of the table stood an elegant silver tureen flanked by etched silver candlesticks.

"It's a really big house," Davy said.

"That it is."

"But it's a mean house."

"A house can't be mean, Davy." Rebecca laid the napkin on the left side of the linen place mat.

"Well, this house is. And it's too quiet, and I don't like it. It's scary. I'm glad the mean man don't want us to stay."

"Doesn't," she said, first correcting his grammar. "Sometimes people are mean because they're sad, Davy." She put the cutglass water goblet in the upper right hand corner of the mat and handed Davy a fork.

He put it down carefully next to the napkin. "Why is he sad?"

"Well, for one thing, he can't walk and run and play the way you and I can." She handed him the knife. "That would make anybody sad, don't you think?"

"I guess." Davy lined up the knife precisely in front of the goblet and reached for the spoon.

"No, Dear, the spoon goes on the outside of the knife, remember?"

He looked up. "Grandpa Spaneas doesn't walk, and he's not mean."

"Grandpa's a lot older than Mr. Fielding."

"I bet Mr. Fielding's guardian angel is real disappointed in him."

Rebecca laughed and tousled Davy's curls. "I'm afraid there are times when we all disappoint our guardian angels." She leaned over and nuzzled his neck, remembering her own self-indulgent tears not long ago.

"I bet he doesn't have very many friends."

"Could be." She picked up the cut-crystal salt and pepper shakers from the butler's chest and returned them to a spot in front of the place setting. She sat down beside Davy and lifted him into her lap. She kissed his ear, raking her fingers gently through his curls. "You know, Darling—we have to forgive folks like Mr. Fielding. He doesn't have a mommy or a daddy to care about him—"

"—and no friends." Davy frowned. Then his face brightened. "He has one."

"And who might that be?" Rebecca gave him a hug.

"Jesus is his friend. Jesus is everybody's friend."

"Well, of course He is. Why didn't I remember that?" She leaned back smiling into her child's face. He was such a serious little boy.

"Maybe he doesn't know. Maybe if we told him, he wouldn't be so mean."

"Somehow I don't think he'd appreciate hearing that from us." Rebecca set Davy back on his feet. "But we can tell him dinner is ready.

"That won't be necessary." Courtney Fielding wheeled into the room.

❧

He had watched it all. From the moment the woman smoothed out the linen place mat and the child laid the spoon so carefully to the right of the knife. He had sat in the shadow of the entry hall and seen her run her fingers through the boy's curls and cuddle him on her lap. And seen that even though her voice was cheerful, her eyes were sad and red from crying.

He'd watched and listened, feeling like a child himself, looking in at a party to which he had not been invited. Feeling like an outsider in his own house.

He ate alone, hearing the soft voices and gentle laughter of the woman and child in the kitchen. The dinner was delicious and temptingly presented. It made a difference. He'd have to remind Neda, who often prepared in haste in order to leave early.

The woman cleared the dishes and poured coffee then returned with a bowl of steaming pudding and a small pitcher of rich cream.

"I don't eat desserts," he said.

Her face fell.

"But perhaps this time I'll make an exception."

His sacrifice was rewarded with a slight smile. She hesitated, waiting until he had taken his first bite.

The pudding was as delicious as it smelled, creamy and rich with spices and now and then the pop of a plump raisin between his teeth. "Very good!"

Satisfied, she turned to leave.

"Mrs. Spaneas—"

"Yes?"

"I talked to my sister. She won't be returning until the end of the summer. Apparently this was her intention all along—which she didn't care to share with me. She also knew Neda would be leaving. It seems you and I have both been duped by Daisy." He wiped his mouth with his napkin. "Of course, this doesn't change anything. But it does give you more time to find appropriate employment elsewhere." He put down his spoon. "In the meantime I think it best to confine your boy's activities to the housekeeper's quarters, the kitchen, and the grounds. He can have full run of the grounds—with appropriate supervision, of course."

"Rest assured, Mr. Fielding—Davy is well supervised."

"No doubt." He could see the defensiveness in her flashing dark eyes. "But I think it best to get parameters clear in the beginning to avoid misunderstandings later."

"Absolutely." She lifted her chin. "And let me also assure you that I expect to earn our keep for as long as we are here. If it's agreeable with you, until I find other employment, I will continue to make your meals and be available to do anything else you need."

"I appreciate that. But there won't be that much to do. The cleaning girl comes during the week and a half day on Saturday." He took another bite of pudding. "Manuel's available if I need him. He's the caretaker and gardener." He polished off the last bite of pudding and pushed his wheelchair back from the table. "Well, I can see I won't starve while you're here." He moved toward the door.

"Mr. Fielding. There is one more thing. Tomorrow is Sunday. Davy and I go to church on Sundays. Could you recommend—"

"I'll give you directions in the morning."

"Thank you."

He was almost to the door.

"Oh, and Mr. Fielding—"

He sighed. "What is it, Mrs. Spaneas?"

"What time do you eat breakfast?"

"Eight o'clock."

ào

Rebecca stood by the door to the butler's pantry and watched Courtney Fielding roll out of the dining room. He was broad through the shoulders, and the play of muscles across his back rippled the fabric of his shirt as he pushed the large wheels that moved his confining chair. Despite his handicap she'd noticed that his trousered legs were long and looked strong, for all their uselessness.

He must have been—must be—quite tall, she thought.

His body was straight and tilted slightly forward, and he pushed with purpose as if he were in a race—or could hardly wait to remove himself from her.

four

"Pancakes are good, Mommy. I want 'em every day, not just Sunday."

"They wouldn't be special if you had them every day." Rebecca finished fastening the last button of Davy's shirt and stood up. Glancing into the clouded bedroom mirror, she straightened the lace collar of her print voile dress, adjusted her straw hat, the one she'd worn yesterday—one of the two she owned—and reached for her purse and Davy's hand.

Together they clattered down the back stairs, through the kitchen, and paused in the sunlit solarium. The wall was all windows and the view breathtaking. A wide carpet of emerald lawn sloped toward the woods lining the arroyo, above which the mauve San Gabriel Mountains shimmered in a hazy morning sun.

Davy pointed to the right. "Look, Mommy—they got a swimming pool. What's the big green thing behind it?"

"That's a tennis court. Every home should have one."

"We didn't have one in the Philippines."

"I was kidding."

"What is it for?"

"It's a game you play with a ball and a racket. Actually Mommy used to be quite good at it in college."

"I like games."

"I know—I'll explain it to you later. We have to hurry now, or we'll be late to church."

She knocked on the library door.

"Come in."

23

Courtney Fielding was sitting by the window. The room was dim and the drapes slightly parted. Through this narrow slice of light he was viewing his world, as he had been the day before when they'd first met. He wheeled his chair around.

"I'm sorry to bother you," Rebecca said. "You were going to give us directions to church."

"I called you a taxi."

"Oh, but I can't afford—"

"I'm taking care of it."

"Davy and I are perfectly capable of—"

"The church is in Eagle Rock. Pastor Jack McCutcheon. I understand they have a good Sunday school." He looked at Davy. "I see George is going to church, too."

Davy nodded.

"Rare to meet a devout monkey these days."

"Devout?"

Courtney Fielding shrugged. "A monkey who says his prayers."

"Oh, yes, George says his prayers every night. He prays for me and Mommy and Daddy in heaven and Grandpa and Gramma Goldie and Auntie Imogene and Uncle—"

"Good for him. I think I hear the cab meter running."

"—and he'll pray for you if you want him to."

"He needn't bother."

"Oh, he doesn't mind at all."

"No!" the man said sharply, then more gently, "No, thank you." He wheeled his chair back toward the window. "Say hello to the pastor for me."

Rebecca shifted her weight. "You know him?"

"We grew up together."

"Maybe—" The last thing Rebecca wanted to do was include this disagreeable man. But it was Sunday. She sighed. And it was the Christian thing to do. Even though she knew it would ruin the day.

She almost gagged, getting the words out. "Maybe. . .you'd like to join us."

"I beg your pardon?" He looked over his shoulder.

"We'd be. . .happy to have you join us."

Courtney Fielding threw back his head and laughed. A harsh, sardonic laugh that hardly sounded like one. "If I were to show up, Jack McCutcheon would drop his teeth. It might just be worth it to see his reaction." He muttered to himself. Then, to Rebecca's profound relief, he added, "I think not."

❧

Davy took the hand of the friendly, scrub-faced young Sunday school teacher and never looked back. With a full heart Rebecca watched him and his stuffed monkey meet the other children, interacting with a poise and openness that many adults didn't possess. Part of it was innate, but part of it was his security in Rebecca's love. He knew she would always be there for him when he returned. Just as she knew her heavenly Father was there for her, regardless of how circuitous the journey.

Well, most of the time she knew it. Sometimes she lapsed, as she had the day before, but not often.

The small church was nearly full when Rebecca entered. She was ushered to one of the last empty seats in a pew near the back. A medley of favorite old hymns floated on a cross-breeze from the open transom windows that ran just below the wood beamed ceiling. She fanned herself with the church bulletin as she studied the simple, whitewashed structure.

The pews and floors were hardwood. A cranberry carpet ran down the center aisle and covered the raised dais below which stood the communion table with an artfully arranged bouquet in the middle of it. Even in the back row the faint perfume of roses reached Rebecca.

Three tapestry-upholstered chairs faced the congregation, a carved pulpit to the left. On the wall behind the choir loft hung a simple wooden cross.

The choir, in their royal blue robes and starched white collars, entered from the left and took their places. The black-robed minister, flanked by two deacons, followed.

Rebecca's eyes widened. She was prepared for the stereotypical pale cleric with the saintly smile. Instead this preacher was young and handsome, a head taller than anyone else on the dais, broad shouldered, tanned, and fit. His rebellious sun-streaked hair struggled to escape its neatly combed part. In fact, he looked as if he spent more time at the beach than behind the pulpit.

The congregation rose, and after a hearty rendition of "Saved by Grace" and a brief invocation, they returned to their seats for the announcements: the potluck supper Wednesday night; the teens' beach outing the following Saturday; the birth of Martha and John Hadley's first child, little Magen Sue, named after her grandmothers, both members of the congregation. "And finally," the deacon reminded them, "don't forget to sign up on the sheet in the narthex to help pack the care packages for the mission orphanages in Europe."

By the time he had finished, Rebecca had a pretty good feeling for what this little church was all about.

She was comforted by the familiarity of the service, the songs, the offering, the doxology—"Praise God from whom all blessings flow. . . ."

The choir stood and sang, "Grace! 'Tis a Charming Sound," and then Pastor Jack McCutcheon rose and stepped to the pulpit. He bowed his head. "Let the words of my mouth, and the meditation of my heart, be acceptable in thy sight, O LORD, my strength, and my redeemer."

His gaze lifted, and for a long moment he scanned the

congregation, as if he were touching each one of them in turn. Then he spread his arms wide.

"Grace!" he proclaimed. "If there is one word that embodies God's blessing, it is grace! Grace is the foundation of our divine heritage."

His deep, resonant baritone vibrated with an energy and conviction that compelled—demanded—anyone within hearing to trust and believe him. He spoke simply and directly, without notes, quoting the Bible verses from memory.

Truly he was a conduit of the Lord, Rebecca thought. She felt of one heart with those in the pews around her. It was easy to see why this small sanctuary was filled to overflowing.

Too soon his sermon rolled toward its conclusion. "It is through His grace that we learn from our mistakes. It is His grace that assures us our prayers will be answered in a way far deeper and greater than we desire or anticipate. God in His grace knows our hearts and our needs far better than we. As the apostle John wrote in John 1:16, 'Of His fulness have all we received, and grace for grace.'"

A beautiful young woman with soulful eyes and brown curly hair rose from the choir and in a soaring soprano sang a capella, "Amazing Grace." The final liquid note seemed to linger on the warm breeze until it was absorbed by the hushed thrall of the breathless congregation.

It was so beautiful. Rebecca felt tears well in her eyes.

And then the congregation rose for the benediction and the final hymn as the choir exited and the young preacher strode down the center aisle.

For the life of her, Rebecca could not remember the benediction or the hymn. All she could think about was the sermon. It was as if she had been sent to this place today to hear this particular message, to be reminded of God's grace in her life. Silently she prayed that grace would include a new position in easy proximity of this sacred spot, for she hoped she had found her church home.

The departing worshippers smiled at her as they passed; some shook her hand while others paused to give a word of welcome. They were so friendly that she suddenly realized she had quite forgotten Davy and hurried out a side door to retrieve him.

When she returned, her son in hand, a few small clusters of people were still left chatting on the front steps. But only one person was ahead of her to greet the pastor, a giggling teenage girl flapping her lashes so hard at the virile young preacher that Rebecca could imagine her suddenly taking flight.

"I can hardly wait until Bible study on Tuesday night, Pastor Jack," she said breathlessly. "You're so—so spiritual. Maybe I can bring cookies for after."

"That would be great, Lauren. I love your chocolate chip cookies."

"Maybe this time I'll bring oatmeal." Flutter. Flutter.

"I'm not sure." Pastor Jack tilted his head and smiled. "Those chocolate chip cookies of yours are pretty special. And maybe you and your fella, Bill, can bring along that unsaved pal of his?"

"I don't know if he—"

Rebecca suppressed a smile. To bring along her "fella" and his "unsaved pal" was clearly not the girl's plan.

"Many a young man found his way to the Lord through chocolate chip cookies, you know, Lauren. And isn't that our mission"—he grasped the girl's hand—"to bring folks to the Lord?"

"I suppose."

"Tuesday night then—you bring along those two fellas and your chocolate chip cookies." He gave her shoulder an affectionate pat as she grudgingly turned toward the street, and he directed his smiling brown eyes on Rebecca. "Welcome, Mrs. Spaneas." He took Rebecca's slender hand in both of his big square ones.

"You know my name?"

"Court called me last night. He told me to look for you this morning." The preacher's eyes were appreciative. "You're just as he described you."

"We invited him to come with us," Rebecca said.

Pastor McCutcheon laughed. "The phone is as close as Court gets to church these days. Even that makes him nervous, I'm afraid. And this must be Davy." The man squatted down to Davy's eye level.

Courtney Fielding had remembered Davy's name? That was a surprise. As far as Rebecca could remember, his only reference had been to "that boy."

"And who is your friend?" Pastor McCutcheon asked.

"This is George," Davy said, thrusting the monkey forward.

The pastor took one of the limp paws and shook it. "How do you do, George?"

He rumpled Davy's hair and rose. "I understand you arrived yesterday," he said to Rebecca.

Rebecca nodded.

The pastor grinned. "And you didn't sleep in this morning? You *are* devout."

A plump middle-aged woman wearing a flowered cloche hat waved and called, "Wonderful message, Pastor Jack."

He waved back.

"Devout. That's what the mean man said George was." Davy looked up at Rebecca. "You know, Mommy, Mr.—Mr.—"

"Mr. Fielding." Rebecca looked chagrined. "He's not mean, Dear. He's just—"

"He makes you cry, Mommy. That's mean."

"We don't need to talk about that now, Davy," she said sternly, not meeting the pastor's gaze.

Pastor McCutcheon shook his head. "It didn't take old Court long to show off his good side, I see." He laid his hand on Davy's head and looked up at Rebecca. "Don't judge him too harshly. I grew up with quite a different man from the one he's turned into since the war. He needs our prayers."

Rebecca nodded.

"Great sermon, Pastor." A ruddy-haired fellow slapped the preacher on the shoulder and ran down the steps to catch up with a woman and a matched pair of boys who looked just like him.

Pastor McCutcheon smiled and turned back to Rebecca.

"Unfortunately, when Mr. Fielding's sister hired me as his housekeeper, she neglected to tell her brother there were two of us," Rebecca said.

"That sounds like Daisy."

"He might have been more receptive had I been alone."

The preacher looked pensive. "I wish you'd known him before. . . . So how do you think it will work out?"

"It won't." Rebecca swallowed the lump that suddenly clogged her throat. "He fired me on the spot."

"You're kidding?"

She forced a smile. "It's not as grim as it sounds. He said I could stay until I found something else."

"Generous of him," the preacher muttered under his breath. He looked thoughtful. "This is a working class congregation. I'm afraid there's not much call for house-keepers, but—"

Rebecca looked embarrassed. "Oh, please, this isn't your problem. You have much more important things to worry about. Besides, you've already helped me. It was as if your sermon this morning were written just for me. When you said God knows our hearts better than we do and that He answers our prayers in ways we can't anticipate. I know it's true, but I needed to be reminded. Your words gave me a great sense of peace."

"I'm happy for that." He smiled warmly. "But I also don't think that God expects us just to sit around and wait for good things to happen. In addition to making this a matter of prayer, Mrs. Spaneas, I intend to make it a matter of action. I do have contacts in other areas—say, can I give you a ride back to Court's? I haven't seen him in over a week. It's time we had a visit."

"That's very kind, Pastor McCutcheon, but I expect your wife will be planning Sunday dinner. Davy and I can—"

"Alas, no wife, Mrs. Spaneas. There aren't many women who want to get by on a pastor's paltry salary." He grinned.

"I doubt that's true. But in that case, yes, Davy and I would welcome a ride back."

"And please, call me Jack."

"Okay, Jack," Davy piped.

"That's Pastor Jack to you, young man," Rebecca said sternly.

five

Responding to a knock on the library door, Court wheeled around his chair to find Jack McCutcheon standing on the threshold. "What are you doing here?"

"Aren't you going to invite me in?"

Court shrugged. "You're already in."

"Thanks for the enthusiasm." Jack strode into the room and dropped onto the couch, stretching his long legs out under the coffee table.

As if he owns the place. Jack was Court's oldest and dearest friend and one of the few he had any desire to see. But sometimes his Christian cheer got on Court's nerves.

"I brought your houseguests home," Jack said, cracking his knuckles.

"That was generous of you."

"She's a very beautiful woman."

"I didn't think preachers noticed that kind of thing."

"I'm not blind." Jack leaned back and crossed his arms. "If she's as nice as she seems, I'd say she was a good choice."

"She wasn't my choice."

"So you said on the phone. But you can always reconsider, you know. She's smart, and she needs the job. She might be willing to stay—if you asked her nicely."

Court gave him a sardonic glance. "Didn't take you long to find out all about her."

Jack shrugged. "I'm a good listener. Wouldn't hurt you to take advantage of my talent. Might even do you some good."

"Thanks for your advice, preacher man."

"My pleasure."

Court stared at him beneath glowering brows. "I give you such trouble. Why do you bother to come here?"

Jack leaned forward. He gazed at his friend in prolonged silence. Finally he said, "I guess it's because I'm waiting for the old Court to—"

"Stand up?" Court's voice was bitter. He looked down at his useless legs and grunted, "You'll have a long wait, Buddy."

"I'm not talking about your legs, Court, and you know it." Jack put his elbows on his knees and clasped his hands.

"Oh, oh. I feel it coming." Court wheeled backward. "If I wanted a sermon, I'd go to church."

"No sermon. Just one old friend to another. I think you should at least give her a try."

"I don't need to. I can see the handwriting on the wall." Court hunkered down in his chair. "Look—I can hardly stand the sound of my own breathing when I get one of my headaches. Can you imagine what it would be like with a kid running through the halls?"

"So close the door and you won't hear him." Jack made a steeple of his hands. "I understand Neda left to help with the new grandchild."

"Mrs. Spaneas told you that too?"

Jack ignored his accusation. "So who'll cook for you if Rebecca leaves?"

"Oh, it's Rebecca now." Court snorted. "Such liberties the clergy are allowed. You want the truth? I wouldn't keep her even without the boy. I can take care of myself. I've done it before. Besides Ada comes every day but Sunday. She can cook for me."

"Be serious, Court. I love the old girl, but Ada cooks about as well as she cleans. All she can make are tuna sandwiches, and they taste like sawdust."

"I can stand them until Daisy comes home."

"Daisy doesn't want to come home," Jack said quietly.

"She's taken care of you and this house long enough. She wants a life of her own. And she's entitled to one."

"She never said that to me," Court said stubbornly.

"She said it by hiring Rebecca."

Court glared at his friend. "Okay, Jack. You've made your point. Maybe eventually I'll need a housekeeper. But not that woman and her boy. If you want to do everyone a favor, find her another job. The sooner the better."

Jack breathed a disappointed sigh and ran a hand through his spiky blond hair. "It'll take time, Court. With all the men coming home, the women are going back to the jobs they did before the war, waitresses, housekeepers. . . . It's not going to be easy for her to find other employment. Especially with the child."

"I understand that. I won't toss her into the streets. I told her so. But I also don't want her to get too comfortable here."

"I assured her I'd do my best to help her. I had just hoped—"

"In the long run she'll be as relieved as I am."

"Don't be so sure. But it's your choice, old friend." Jack looked over at him. "Believe it or not, there are a lot of people who care about you. You just don't choose to accept it." He reached out and touched Court's knee. "There's one in particular—"

"Don't say it." Court shrugged his hand away. "Don't bring God into this."

"He's in it whether you want Him there or not."

"That's your opinion," Court said sharply.

For a moment Jack looked as if he was going to pursue the subject then thought better of it. "I'm hungry," he said abruptly. "How about you?"

"I could eat something," Court said. "There's leftover meatloaf in the refrigerator."

"I'm taking you to Sunday dinner."

Court wheeled his chair back. "You know I don't like to go out."

"I'll wager you haven't eaten out since you and Daisy and I went to that Mexican joint two months ago." Jack came to his feet.

"And Daisy got sick on the chicken enchiladas," Court reminded him. "Reason enough to stay out of restaurants."

"No Mexican joint today. We're going upscale."

"Since when can you afford upscale?" Court said. "I thought your salary came from what was in the collection plate."

"It does. Who says *I'm* paying?" Jack stepped behind the wheelchair and began pushing Court toward the door.

"Cut it out." Court grabbed the wheel, stopping the chair's forward motion with a jolt. "I'm perfectly capable of navigating myself."

"But are you willing?"

Court thought about it a minute then breathed a beleaguered sigh. "Very well. Let me put on a tie and jacket. I'll be down in a minute."

❧

Rebecca hurried into the entry hall, her hat in her hand, Davy at her heels. "Oh, Jack, I am so sorry. I don't know where I buried my brain. I can't go out. I have to prepare dinner for Mr. Fielding."

Courtney Fielding wheeled out of the elevator. "No, you don't. Jack and I are going out to dinner."

"I invited Rebecca and Davy to go with us," Jack said.

Courtney Fielding's face reflected surprise.

Rebecca said quickly, "Davy and I can rustle up something here. Maybe some of that lovely meatloaf from last night, if that's all right, Mr. Fielding."

"We wouldn't hear of it, Rebecca. Would we, Court?" The minister glanced at his friend for confirmation.

"Absolutely not."

Still, Rebecca caught the glance of irritation Courtney Fielding directed at his friend.

It was an awkward moment. Only Jack, who had orchestrated the whole thing, looked untroubled. And Davy, who was walking his monkey George on top of the cherry-wood table in the middle of the entry hall.

"Can George come?" he asked Jack.

"By all means."

"He likes to sit up at the counter."

"I'm afraid there is no counter where we're going, but he can order whatever he wants to eat."

Courtney Fielding turned his flashing cobalt eyes on Jack. "It's settled then," he said impatiently and wheeled toward the front door.

"But—" Rebecca looked helplessly at the pastor.

He shrugged then smiled and offered her his arm.

She stood undecided. She felt embarrassed. She knew Mr. Fielding did not welcome her or Davy's company. Even if he hadn't meant to show it, his expressive face could not hide his annoyance.

But as much as Mr. Fielding did not want them, it appeared Jack did.

Rebecca pursed her lips. She saw through Jack's good intentions, but they were misguided.

Courtney Fielding's shoulders hunched as he wheeled down the ramp on the far side of the front stairs.

"Come on, Mommy. Let's go." Davy tugged at her hand.

With considerable apprehension Rebecca took the pastor's arm. This had all the elements of a miserable afternoon.

❧

As the minister had promised, the restaurant was definitely upscale. They were seated in the Garden Room, surrounded on three sides by windows that overlooked a meandering stream in a sylvan setting of ferns and flowers.

With a four year old beside her, the sight of pristine linen cloths and napkins, sterling settings and cut-crystal goblets did not bode well. Rebecca's distressing expectations were not only met; they were exceeded.

Three times during the first half hour she had to excuse herself to take Davy to the rest room. A new record, even for him. Once was on urgent business; the second time was to wash off the olive juice he'd dribbled down the front of his shirt when he'd popped olives on all five fingers, like a line of finger puppets, then eaten them one by one.

But the coup de grâce was when he reached for a roll and knocked over his glass of tomato juice. It spread across the white linen cloth like a bloody stain, splashing red spots on Courtney Fielding's beige linen jacket.

Davy began to whimper.

People at nearby tables turned to look, some in sympathy, others with irritation.

If Rebecca had tried to conjure a disastrous meal, she could hardly have imagined worse. When she rose for yet another trip to the rest room, she saw the look that passed between Courtney Fielding and Pastor Jack and knew the final nail had been hammered into the coffin of her fate in the Fielding household.

Then, to her utter amazement, Courtney Fielding began to laugh. "And we're only on the appetizer." He leaned forward and ruffled Davy's hair. "And what entertainment have you planned for the entrée, my friend?"

Abruptly Davy stopped crying. His mouth dropped open.

At that moment the waiter hurried up, all apologies, as if he'd been responsible, and laid clean napkins over the stain.

"Remember when you spilled the catsup at Bob's Big Boy, Jack?" Courtney Fielding grinned.

"And the ensuing catsup fight?" Jack laughed. "I sure do. As I recall, the manager threw us out."

"Don't give the boy ideas." Their host glanced at Davy.

"We were seventeen, not four," Jack reminded him with chagrin. "As I recall, Daisy and her date were in the thick of things." He grinned. "That kid sister of yours always was trouble."

"We were with the Lombardy girls," Courtney Fielding mused. He turned to Rebecca. "Jack and I have always had an affinity for the same women. We lucked out with them. They were identical twins."

"I can't remember—after that incident did they ever go out with us again?" Jack asked.

Courtney Fielding looked smug. "I didn't want to tell you, but—"

"Aha."

"I wasn't quite sure which one of the twins it was. The one you had dated or the one I dated." He looked sly. "But I remember thinking at the time that I didn't recognize the way she kissed, so she must have been yours."

For the moment Courtney Fielding seemed to have transcended his affliction or momentarily forgotten it. He raked back a shock of dark hair with long, lean fingers. His amazing blue eyes crinkled with laughter. His teeth gleamed in a wide smile. Rebecca could see the outline of his broad shoulders and muscled arms beneath the beige linen jacket—albeit embellished with red tomato-juice spots.

He was handsome. For the first time since they'd met, she realized how handsome. She understood now why her sister, Imogene, had written home before the war about her crush on her best friend Daisy's older brother.

In those days Courtney Fielding must have really been something to write home about.

six

The waiter interrupted Rebecca's contemplation by serving the entrée, a classic Sunday dinner of crispy fried chicken, mashed potatoes and gravy, fresh peas and biscuits—the plate garnished with a sprig of parsley in this "upscale" restaurant.

"George don't like peas," Davy announced.

"Doesn't," Rebecca corrected quietly. "George *doesn't* like peas."

"I'm with George," Courtney Fielding said.

"Thanks. That really helps." Rebecca gave him a sidelong smile. She turned to Davy. "You eat your half of the peas, and you can leave George's half on the plate." Much to her relief Davy created no further problem, and the dinner continued with pleasant conversation and the men's past reminiscences into which she was drawn.

The waiter had cleared the dishes and was just serving dessert when a large, ruddy-faced man in a plaid sports jacket—the kind worn by a fellow who plays golf on Sundays instead of going to church—paused by their table. "Jack? Court?" He had the gravelly voice of a long-time smoker.

"Herb Brown!" Jack began to rise.

"Don't get up!" the man boomed, touching his shoulder. "I thought I recognized you guys. How long has it been? Twelve, fifteen years?"

"At least." Jack turned to Rebecca. "Herb is an old friend of ours from high school. Herb, this is Mrs. Spaneas and her son, Davy."

Rebecca smiled. "How do you do?"

"Good to see you, Herb." Courtney Fielding shook his hand.

Rebecca noticed that his smile was thin. There was something in his expression that made her feel as if he were pulling into himself.

"What are you doing in these parts?" Jack asked.

"Taking the old folks out for Sunday dinner."

Davy curled closer to Rebecca and whispered, "That man's got a awful loud voice."

"Shh."

But Herb Brown seemed not to notice. "You guys look great." He turned to Rebecca. "The two musketeers, we used to call 'em. Always together. What one didn't shine in, the other did, athletics, scholastics. Even with the dolls."

"You had dolls, Mr. Court?" Davy asked.

"He means girls, Davy," Jack said.

"Like my mommy."

"Oh, no, little fellah." The blustery man lifted his lips, showing his teeth to Rebecca the way a monkey does when it's about to bite into a banana. "Your mom isn't a doll. She's a real classy lady. But, hey"—he turned his attention back to Jack—"what's with that collar? Don't tell me you're a preacher."

"You guessed it." Jack grinned.

"The way you horsed around? You're about the last kid I would have picked. Now Court here, he's another story." The man laughed. "Remember, Court, how you used to pray before every game? Some of us guys got pretty impatient with you. To put it mildly. If you were gonna pray, we thought you should at least pray to win." He turned to Rebecca. "But, oh, no, not old Court. He'd pray we'd all do our best and that no one would get hurt. And that went for the opponents as well."

Court didn't respond.

"In spite of it we usually managed to win," Jack pointed out.

Herb Brown shook his head and for an instant was silent, as if he were playing it all back in his mind. He sighed. "A lot of water over the dam since those days, the war and all. I remember you lucky guys got to see action."

Courtney Fielding's hands tightened on the armrests of his wheelchair.

"I worked for Lockheed," the man said.

"That was a job that needed doing just as much, Herb," Jack assured him. "You probably built the plane I flew in."

"Could be. But when you're a young guy, rarin' to get into the fray. . . . I tried to enlist, but they wouldn't take me. Bad back." He grinned. "Never affected my golf game, though." For an instant he looked heavenward. "Thank You! Unlike Court, I pray to win—you guys look great. Court still looks like a linebacker with those shoulders."

"I was the linebacker," Jack said. "Court was the quarterback."

"Oh, yeah," the man boomed on without missing a breath. "Hey, are you still playing tennis, Court?" He looked at Rebecca. "Let me tell you about this guy. He played on championship teams in three sports. He was California *champion* in tennis—so, Court, have you kept it up?"

Courtney Fielding looked down at the dish of melting orange sherbet in front of him. "Oh, yeah."

"Maybe we can get up a game sometime. Where do you play?"

"At the veterans' hospital."

The man looked puzzled. "They have tennis courts there?"

"Table tennis. I'm table tennis champion. You know how it goes, once an athlete, always an athlete."

"Table tennis?" He looked at Jack. "Is he puttin' me on?" And then he noticed the handgrips on the back of Court's wheelchair. His ruddy face turned florid. "Oh, no. I'm sorry. I didn't notice. . . ."

"Don't worry about it," Courtney Fielding said.

Herb Brown shook his head. "That's awful. How did it happen?"

The murmur of the surrounding voices and the clink of cutlery on china seemed to increase in volume as an awkward quiet dropped over the table. No one quite knew where to look. . .or what to say.

"Hey, Mr. Court, your orange sherbet looks like soup," Davy observed, breaking the silence.

"I can't tell you how sorry I am," the man muttered.

"Forget it." Court glanced at Jack.

"I don't know what I would have done in your place." He cleared his throat.

Courtney Fielding stared at his clasped hands.

"Well—ah—they've probably brought the car around. The folks will wonder where I am. You remember my folks."

"Sure do." Jack rose and extended his hand. "Your mom made the best pecan pie west of the Mississippi. Say hello to them for me."

"Will do. Nice meeting you, Mrs. Spaneas, Davy. Great seeing you guys again. Now that we've hooked up, maybe we can get together. Like old times. . . ."

Rebecca noticed the subtle technique preachers have perfected: as Jack shook the man's hand he moved him along toward the door.

She didn't want to look at Courtney Fielding, and yet she couldn't help herself. His elbows were on the armrests of his wheelchair. He clenched and unclenched his fists as a montage of raw emotion played across his handsome face, bitterness, self-loathing, loneliness. She felt drawn to him, perhaps because of the pain she saw there. She had seen so much of it, lived through so much of it, experienced so much of it herself.

But she was one of the lucky ones. She still had a scar; she always would. But, for the most part, she had healed. Much of that was due to a loving and supportive family and her precious Davy. But especially her belief in God.

She could only imagine the turmoil and suffering of the man beside her. Courtney Fielding was maimed and lonely. Where was the faith Herb Brown had said came so easily to him as a young man?

She wanted to reach out and touch him, tell him that he was whole in God's sight. And loved. That God had never left him and was waiting, as a loving father waits, for His child to return.

Of course she couldn't tell him that. It would have been unacceptable, crass. A perfect stranger having the audacity. But oddly she didn't feel like a stranger. The journey on which her own suffering had taken her had given her insight and compassion for the suffering of others. For his suffering. As she sat beside him, within the dissonance of activity that surrounded them, she breathed a silent prayer that his heart would be opened to the blessings that were available to him.

Jack returned and dropped back into his chair. "That Herb Brown always was a big talker—without a whole lot to say, I'm afraid."

Davy whispered to his mother, "If Mr. Court don't want his orange sherbet soup, can I have it?"

Rebecca shook her head. "You've had enough."

Abruptly Courtney Fielding pushed his wheelchair back from the table. "It's been two years; you'd think I'd get over it," he mumbled. He swung the chair around and maneuvered toward the door with the agile ferocity of an athlete determined to outrace his adversary. Only in this case he, himself, was the adversary.

seven

The twenty-minute drive home from the restaurant seemed interminable. Sitting in the front seat next to Jack, Court made no pretense of pleasantness, leaving that to him and Mrs. Spaneas, with periodic observations from Davy.

As Court waited for Jack to retrieve his wheelchair from the trunk of the car, his feeling of helplessness intensified with the painful awareness of Mrs. Spaneas's compassionate gaze from the seat behind him. He did not want or need her sympathy. All he wanted was to be left alone. When he'd acquiesced, at Jack's insistence, to have Sunday dinner, his instincts had told him it was a mistake. When he saw Mrs. Spaneas and Davy in the hall, he was certain of it.

Then those brief moments at dinner when he'd not thought of his affliction, when he'd laughed and bantered with his old friend, encouraged by their charming companion and her small son. The contrast was more cruel when he was slapped back into reality by the unwelcome arrival of Herb Brown. Herb Brown, of all people. A fellow with whom he'd had so little in common in high school he'd forgotten his name.

Jack opened the car door.

Without a word Court hefted himself into the chair and wheeled up the ramp, paused to unlock the front door and pushed himself into the mansion.

❧

Rebecca and Jack exchanged glances as he helped her out of the car, their thoughts about Courtney Fielding clear but unspoken. Davy slid across the seat after his mother, hopped

44

onto the cobbled drive and ran ahead of them toward the north lawn, dragging George along with him.

"That monkey needs a bath more often than Davy," Rebecca said. "Unfortunately he rarely gets one. It's like pulling teeth to get George out of my son's hands." She removed her hat and tucked a strand of dark hair back into her French roll. "I guess every child needs a best friend. George is Davy's." She smiled up at her tall companion. "I learn a lot about what Davy's thinking from eavesdropping on their conversations."

Jack touched her elbow, steering her toward a bench near the tennis court. "I can't imagine how difficult it must be raising a child in the midst of war."

"It was, and it wasn't," Rebecca said. "It's hard on us adults because we know the terrible possibilities. Children don't. They accept the chaos as part of their daily routine." Her gaze followed Davy as he hopped through the afternoon shadows and rolled down the sloping lawn. "They take it for granted that God is watching over them and will protect them."

"We adults could take a page from their book, I reckon," Jack said.

The two had reached the bench.

"Davy, I'm over here!" Rebecca called. "Stay where you can see me."

He waved back.

She smiled and sat down, laying her hat next to her purse on the bench beside her. "And of course Davy has the added security of his wonderful daddy keeping an eye on him."

Jack dropped down beside her. "Your husband—"

"—was killed right after the Japanese invaded the Philippines. Davy wasn't born yet."

"He never knew his father then." The pastor's warm brown eyes were filled with empathy.

"Only what he's learned from me." Rebecca never thought of what her son had missed without sadness sweeping through her.

For a minute she stared thoughtfully at the green grass beneath her feet. Jack sat silent beside her, turning to look out at the sweeping vista.

Ruefully she said, "I know everyone has imperfections, but David Spaneas didn't live long enough for me to discover his."

"He must have been a very special person," Jack said.

"He was. He was a man of the highest principles. And he was brilliant. A university professor. I was very lucky to have had him for even that brief time." She sighed. "And very lucky to have him as an example for our son." She lifted her eyes and met Jack's compassionate gaze. "I feel as if he's with me—"

"Watching over you, too."

"More than that. He's still my husband. He always will be. I cannot imagine ever being married to anyone else."

≈

From the library window Court gazed through the partially parted drapes and watched the child scamper through the shadows, laughing, falling spread-eagle on the grass, rolling over and over, then repeating the process. He wondered how he could manage it so many times without getting dizzy.

He'd followed the progress of Jack and Mrs. Spaneas as they strolled across the north lawn toward the tennis court, Davy hopping around them like an excited bunny. He'd watched Mrs. Spaneas remove her hat and smooth her hair and Jack grab playfully for the boy as he darted past.

His eyes drifted back to her now, sitting on the bench beside his friend.

A cloak of envy spread over Court, so heavy his shoulders sagged from the weight of it. He turned from the window, sick at heart.

When he and Jack were young, sharing interests and competition had been the glue that held them together and the impetus that drove them to succeed. The two musketeers. They had challenged each other and brought out the best. But they had also reveled in each other's accomplishments. Their ambition had been tempered by love, not envy.

Now, Court feared, envy was the sword that was about to divide them, and he seemed helpless to control it.

Jack would never see the gleam of that sword, or if he did, he wouldn't recognize it as such. Not when it came to his friend, Court. He was a realist, but he viewed the world through the filter of God's love and always viewed Court with the acceptance of his generous heart.

Court glanced again through the window.

The bench on which Jack and Mrs. Spaneas sat was under the old oak that shaded the studio. The studio that Court's gaze avoided and in which his spirit was buried.

He saw Jack lean forward, giving the woman his full attention, and wondered what they were talking about. Was he, Court, part of their conversation? *What are we going to do with poor old Court?*

He was thinking too much. The woman started it. Why had Daisy hired her? To torment him. Typical. Of course it wasn't so; it just felt that way. He'd manage all right with his sister gone. Even better. He wouldn't have to suffer her nagging about what was good for him. *Get out into the world; meet people.*

He met plenty of people, cripples like him, at the VA hospital.

❧

Jack looked up at the library window. "He's so isolated. Today was the first time he's been out in months. A good sign, until—" He shook his head.

"It's a shame," Rebecca said. "Especially when it doesn't have to be that way." She sighed. "Easy enough for me to say."

"I wish you could have known him before the war. Just the opposite of what he is now." The minister balanced his elbows on his knees and hunched over his folded hands. "He was my best friend. He still is."

"He's lucky to have you."

Jack sat back on the bench. "I've been lucky to have him. When I was in college I turned real wild, liquor, girls—not the kind we dated in high school—"

"Like the Lombardy twins."

He grinned. "Well. . ."

"So Court wasn't perfect either."

"Not perfect, maybe, but good. Down to the bottom of his boots. He was more grounded than the rest of us. Even when his parents were killed."

"Oh, no."

"An airplane accident. He was a freshman in college at the time, and Daisy was still in high school."

"How tragic."

"But he stayed strong for her, and if his faith faltered, I never saw it." Jack crossed his arms. A faraway look came into his eyes. "I remember the day he brought me to the Lord. He stood beside me at the front of the church, his hand on my shoulder. His hand was warm and strong and felt—it felt the way I imagined Jesus' hand must have felt." He let out a long breath. "Court never gave up on me, and I'm not about to give up on him."

Davy ran up, the grass-stained George dangling from his hand. "Hey, Mommy, George and me is thirsty."

Rebecca rose and took her son's hand. "We'll get you a drink in the kitchen."

As she and Jack strolled back toward the house, she asked, "What happened to him? How was he injured?"

"In Italy. He was on a reconnaissance mission. Especially dangerous. Court had volunteered. That was typical of him."

Jack thrust his hands into his trouser pockets. "They said he had no trouble assembling a platoon. He'd proved himself. Brave but not foolhardy. Good judgment. The men trusted him." He paused, absently studying the toe of his shoe. "That was Court."

The pastor began walking again, Rebecca beside him. Davy dragged at her hand as he bent over, searching the lawn for worms.

Jack continued. "They were behind enemy lines. They'd gotten the information they'd been sent to find and were on their way back—when they were ambushed." As he spoke, his square, tanned face reflected the depth of his emotion. "Four of the six died where they stood. Court and another were wounded. It seems Court still managed to drag his comrade to safety. Then he collapsed. He hasn't walked since."

They had reached the back steps. Davy drew away from his mother, pulled open the back door and ran into the house, letting the door slam behind him.

"As it turns out," Jack said, "he was dragging a dead man."

"Oh, no." The horror and sadness of it. Rebecca shook her head. Pausing at the bottom of the steps, she turned to the pastor, perplexed. "If he was so severely wounded as to still be crippled, how did he manage to—"

"During the war I saw men do amazing feats under extreme pressure. Apparently he was in excruciating pain. When they operated, they found that a piece of shrapnel had only nicked his spine." Jack pulled open the door. His gaze met hers. "They expected him to have a full recovery."

"Which implies—"

Jack shrugged. "I'm not a doctor."

Rebecca drew water from the tap for Davy's drink and leaned against the counter, looking up at the man as he made the small talk that wound down their conversation.

As seemed his habit, he'd shoved his hands into his trouser pockets. "As I said this morning, I'll make some phone calls about a job for you."

"I really appreciate that." She took the empty glass from Davy and set it on the sink. "I have such limited resources—actually none."

"Don't worry. It may take some time, but we'll find just the right thing for you. Have faith."

"That's about all I can afford to have." Rebecca gave him a sheepish smile.

Jack's face turned serious. "Of course, the best thing that could happen would be for you to stay here."

"I won't stay where I'm not wanted."

"Don't take it personally. I don't think Court knows what he wants. But I understand how you feel." He gave her a crooked smile. "I was thinking of what was best for Court, not you and Davy."

"Davy! Oh, where is he?" Rebecca glanced quickly around the kitchen. "Davy?" she called—but not too loud. "Oh, dear. Mr. Fielding was adamant that Davy not be allowed to run through the house. Believe me, I agree." She rushed toward the door leading into the solarium. "I wouldn't want to suffer the consequences if he broke something. Then I'm afraid we *would* be out in the street."

She found him in the solarium about to pick up a Miessen bird, its porcelain beak piercing the heart of a lily.

"It looks like a hummingbird, Mommy."

"Don't touch it, Davy." Rebecca reached out. As she grabbed the antique figurine from her son's hands, it slipped through her fingers, shattering on the tile floor.

The three stared at the shards of the once priceless porcelain scattered in front of them. Even Davy could not speak.

"Fe fi fo fum. I smell—blood!" a voice boomed from the doorway.

As one, Jack, Rebecca and Davy lifted their eyes.

"Oh, Mr. Fielding, I'm so sorry." Rebecca was on the brink of tears. "Please don't blame Davy. It wasn't his—"

"Don't get angry at the boy, Court." Jack stepped forward.

Courtney Fielding held up his hand for silence.

Davy pressed back against his mother's legs.

All eyes were on Courtney Fielding as he pushed his wheelchair into the room and up to the side table on which the artifact once sat. He picked up its porcelain companion, a bird with its beak in a rose, studied it for a moment then deliberately dropped it.

In stunned silence the other three gazed down at the smashed shards commingling on the tile floor.

Courtney Fielding lifted his gaze. "I never could stand those cutesy dust-catchers. Daisy won't be happy, but"—he looked at Davy through narrowed eyes—"I won't tell her who broke them if you won't."

Davy looked up at Rebecca. "I won't tell on you, Mommy."

"*You* were the culprit?" Courtney Fielding lifted astonished eyes.

She nodded. "That's what we were trying to tell you."

"I could have saved myself the trouble," he muttered, spinning his wheelchair around. At the door he paused and turned, facing the room again. "So what took you so long to get back to the house?" He looked at Rebecca. "Was my *loyal* friend filling you in on my life's story?"

Rebecca glanced at Jack.

"I can see by your expression that he was. Did he also tell you the doctors think I'm crazy? Not dangerous. Just crazy. I see not. That's for another day." He spun his chair around for the final time. Over his shoulder he said, "When you and the good pastor have said your good-byes, Mrs. Spaneas, please come into the library."

eight

Since she'd arrived, approximately twenty-four hours before, three times Rebecca had been obliged to knock on the library door, and each time her stomach had roiled with the nausea of apprehension. Courtney Fielding couldn't be any more anxious to get rid of her than she was to leave. Now, with the fragmentation of the precious porcelain, the ax would surely fall. If she only had somewhere else to go, she might have initiated the exit herself.

To make matters worse, if it were possible, even when she left, that would not be the end of it. She was an honorable woman and determined to pay for the broken figurine—whatever it cost—insuring her financial bondage to Courtney Fielding until she did. At least, by leaving, she wouldn't have to endure his somber visage on a daily basis.

He responded to her knock. "Come in."

Rebecca took a deep breath and pushed open the door.

From behind the desk he looked up at her through a pair of horn-rimmed reading glasses. He was in his shirtsleeves, his tie loosened. "Ah, Mrs. Spaneas."

Whom else did he expect?

"Please sit down." His voice sounded ominously pleasant. He gestured toward the straight-back leather chair in front of the desk. "We have finances to discuss."

"I assure you, Mr. Fielding, I fully intend to pay for the broken figurine." Rebecca lowered herself onto the edge of the chair, poised for flight.

"I assure *you*, Mrs. Spaneas, if I required that, you would be in servitude to me for considerably more time than either of us wants. No, we'll forget the figurine." He looked over the rim of his glasses. "To be honest, they were my grandmother's, and I never did like them much. I'd rather have the insurance."

So much for sentiment. "I don't feel right—"

"Please." He raised his hand for her silence. "We have a more pressing matter to discuss. While you're here and assuming the duties of housekeeper, you should be appropriately compensated." He looked down at the sheet of paper in front of him on the desk. "I just found a note in that regard left by Daisy." He frowned and slid the paper across the desk to Rebecca. "*This* is what she offered?"

Rebecca glanced at the paper and nodded.

When she had agreed to the contract, she'd realized that it was barely enough to make ends meet. But she was anxious to get stateside and, with no other options, had accepted the terms, concluding optimistically that once her employer saw the quality of her work, in due time he would give her a raise. Of course that was a moot point now. If Courtney Fielding had his way—and she had hers, for that matter—she wouldn't be here that long.

He shook his head. "I can't believe it. Daisy never did have any sense about money. That's what comes of never having to earn a living."

Rebecca could hardly believe it. The man was quibbling about a paltry twenty-five dollars a week.

"This amount is an insult," he said.

It is indeed! Rebecca straightened. "Don't worry," she said curtly. "Davy and I will be satisfied with board and room until I find other employment." What better incentive than living at the poverty level.

"I'm surprised you accepted it," he said, as if she hadn't spoken. "You could not possibly support yourself and the boy on this amount. If you're worth anything, you're worth twice as much."

Was she hearing right?

"I might suggest you keep that in mind when negotiating with your future employer." He took off his glasses and laid them on the desk. "In the meantime you'll receive fifty dollars a week."

It was so unexpected; it took a moment for Rebecca to collect herself. "Thank you very much. I'm—I'm very grateful."

"You needn't be. Fair is fair." He shrugged. "I expect you'll earn it."

He didn't look nearly as disagreeable as he had, or as formal, with his shirtsleeves rolled up—nor as intimidating when he'd taken off his glasses and almost smiled. "Ada, the maid, will be here tomorrow morning," he said. "She usually arrives about eight-thirty—if her arthritis isn't acting up. Her grandson, Paul, drops her off and drives me to therapy. I take my breakfast at seven forty-five on weekdays." He raked back the shock of dark hair that seemed habitually to fall across his brow. "That's pretty much my schedule. Any questions?"

Rebecca thought for a moment. "Since I'll be doing the cooking, is there anything special you like to eat?"

"Whatever you fix will be fine."

She squirmed, glancing from his face to the wheelchair in which he sat. It was an awkward moment, but she felt she had to ask. "Ah—is there anything special *you* require?"

He frowned and straightened. "I'll let you know if there is." His tone was brusque. By calling attention to his disability, the congenial mood had been abruptly broken.

He reached over and picked up a folded sheet of newspaper lying at the corner of the desk. "I cut out the want ads from this morning's paper. Circled some I thought might interest you." He handed it to her.

No doubt as to his ultimate intention—despite the additional compensation, this was still temporary employment.

❧

The following morning Rebecca was clearing up the dishes—with the help of Davy and George—when a small, stooped old lady in a faded aqua-blue uniform and wide nurse's shoes shuffled from the back porch into the kitchen. Around her head was tied a red and white bandana from which sprang tufts of thin gray hair.

Grunting, she deposited a large black handbag by the chair at the end of the kitchen table and looked up. One rheumy blue eye assessed Rebecca from beneath sparse brows then softened as it set on Davy. "You must be the new house-keeper." Her thin, high voice crackled like two live wires touching. "And who is your helper?"

"I'm Rebecca Spaneas. This is my son, Davy." *Surely she isn't the maid.*

Davy shrank back from the old lady's extended blue-veined hand.

"Don't worry, young dear. I'm not a wicked witch. Although at my age I might look like one."

Rebecca ventured hesitantly. "Ada Denglar?"

"You got it." The old lady gave a cackly laugh. "Had you fooled, too, didn't I?" Patting Davy on the head, she pulled a peppermint ball from the pocket of her dress and offered it to him. "Never without 'em, don't you know. At eighty-two, if I'm not careful, my breath could clear a room."

Davy gave his mother a quavering look. When she nodded her permission, he reached out, grabbed the mint and, in a single motion, whipped off the cellophane wrapper and popped it into his mouth.

"Not so fast, young man." Rebecca squeezed his shoulder. "What do you say?"

He whispered a moist thank-you, the peppermint ball rolling over his tongue.

"First things first." Ada Denglar shuffled over to the stove, checked to see if the teakettle had water in it and turned on the burner. She shuffled back to the table, lowered herself halfway and dropped with a thump into the chair. "The tea pot and cups are over there." She gestured to a cupboard to the right of the sink. "The tea's above the stove. I take sugar and milk in mine." She looked at Davy. "How do you like yours?"

"Mommy doesn't let me drink tea," he said, forgetting his shyness.

"A little milk tea never hurt nobody. In fact it's good for you." She reached in her bag. "Just happened to have these for dipping to go with it." She pulled out a small box of frosting-filled chocolate cookies.

Davy looked at them longingly. "Mommy doesn't let me have cookies for breakfast, neither."

Ada Denglar glanced at the kitchen clock sitting on the shelf above the stove. "I had breakfast an hour ago, so we're safe."

Some people had a real sense of entitlement when it came to badgering and bossing other people around, Rebecca thought, glancing at the back of the woman's head. But Davy seemed charmed by her. Judging from the expression on his face he was having his first really happy experience in this somber house.

"Now, little dear, tell me about yourself," Ada Denglar said, leaning forward.

The little boy needed scant prodding. The avid interest reflected in the old lady's lined face was encouragement enough. As Rebecca set out the cups, poured tea into the pot to steep, and retrieved the cream from the refrigerator, he told, with some embellishment from her, the chronicle of his short life (what he could remember of it) up to the time they left the Philippines. He continued with a dissertation on all his beloved relatives and the trip across the Pacific. And finally he told her how, at the journey's end, he met Mr. Court, who he and George still weren't convinced was all that nice, especially when he made Davy's mother cry and said he didn't want them living here even though they had hardly lived here at all anyway.

Ada Denglar shook her head. "Poor Mr. Court. It's true. He isn't the same man he once was. But there's a reason."

There's always a reason, Rebecca thought, as she poured tea into two of the cups. *But some folks manage to rise above it.* Davy's cup she filled by a quarter and added milk to the top.

Ada Denglar poured herself cream and spooned a generous helping of sugar into hers and Davy's tea. "That'll fix what ails you." She opened the box of cookies and allowed him two, "One for each hand," before offering them to Rebecca.

Rebecca shook her head. "No, thank you."

"Leaves more for us." The woman winked her good eye at Davy.

Didn't she know anything about nutrition? Very much time in her company and Davy's teeth will be rotted out.

At that moment a round young man, almost as short as Ada and looking very much like her, poked his head through the door from the solarium. "I'm taking Mr. Court to his therapy, Grandma." He glanced at Rebecca and smiled. "He says the VA bus will bring him home by lunchtime."

"Tell him I'll have a tuna sandwich waiting," his grandmother called as the door swung closed. She turned to Rebecca. "Mr. Court's favorite. Loved my tuna sandwiches since he was Davy's age." She took a sip of tea. "This was Mr. Court's grandmother's house, you know. He and Daisy came to live here when their folks were killed. So sad."

Rebecca nodded, warming her hands around the cup. "Pastor Jack told me about it."

"Then, of course, when she died, the house was theirs."

Davy split open one of his cookies and began licking the cream filling off one side.

"Sixty-two years since I began working for the old Mrs. Fielding. I was just a girl. I've seen a lot happen in this house since then. Death, taxes, and two world wars. Fortunately I don't have to worry about taxes." She brushed off the crumbs that had collected on her bosom. "Well, time to get to work." Her bones creaked as she rose. She took a staggering step holding onto the back of the chair, got her balance and began stacking the plates.

Rebecca couldn't bear it. She jumped to her feet. "Let me do the dishes, Mrs. Denglar."

"No! It's my job," the woman said sternly. "I may be crippled with arthritis, blind in one eye, and have a heart condition. I may be slow. But I'm steady—and strong as I need to be. And as for cleaning, what my good eye misses isn't worth seeing anyway." Her laugh sounded like a flock of chickens clucking over fresh feed as she made her way over and put the dishes in the sink. While she waited for the water to heat in the tap, she said, "I have to work, don't you know. I owe Mr. Court too much not to."

"You owe him?"

"If I lived to be a hundred I wouldn't earn enough to pay that man back." She gave another cackly laugh. "And let's face it, a hundred ain't far away."

Rebecca was appalled. She'd begun to soften her attitude toward the man when he'd increased her wages. *Fair is fair. Isn't that what he'd said?* But she couldn't see one thing fair about a rich man like Courtney Fielding heartlessly taking advantage of an ailing old woman. Why, the poor old thing was no better than an indentured servant.

Ada Denglar poured soap flakes into the dishpan and swished her hand in it to make bubbles. "As long as I can listen to 'Our Gal Sunday' and 'Portia Faces Life' on the radio while I work, I'm happy. It gives me a perspective, don't you know." Her lined face broke into a smile. "I figure if Portia, with all her troubles, can face life, I certainly should be able to."

Rebecca smiled. Ada Denglar was the one note of grace in this otherwise sad symphony. She picked up a dishtowel and began drying the dishes.

"By the way," the old woman said, "call me Ada."

nine

For the next three weeks, five days a week and a half day on Saturday, Ada hobbled into the house and went through her morning routine.

With each day Rebecca's indignation grew.

She was just waiting, counting the hours, when she could tell Courtney Fielding what she thought of his thoughtless treatment of Ada. Every time she saw the old dear struggle to push the heavy vacuum or wheeze up the endless winding staircase lugging her pail of cleaning equipment or clutch her hip in arthritic pain, Rebecca's ire grew. Oh, she could hardly wait to tell him. But until she had found other gainful employment, she was forced to hold her tongue.

She felt like a hypocrite.

She herself tried to assume as many of Ada's chores as she could, without wounding the proud woman's pride. But if Ada even suspected an intrusion into what she considered her domain, Rebecca was told to mind her own business and let Ada mind hers, in just so many words.

Each day, after Ada had gone home, Rebecca inspected, catching those spots that Ada's one good eye had missed. She had no intention of giving their employer an opportunity to criticize the old lady. He appeared to be generally indifferent to what went on in the household, but one never knew.

It seemed to Rebecca that he was especially remote with her. Their exchanges brief and to the point. Since that Sunday in the restaurant she had rarely seen a smile.

Sad. It was such a handsome smile.

Ada's obvious devotion to him did give her pause. Although she saw very little lovable about the man, something must be there—or had been. Then one morning Ada pulled a photograph album out of her large black satchel and opened it before them on the kitchen table.

Slowly she turned the pages. A smile crinkled the lines of her face as she pointed her gnarled finger at the various pictures, reminiscing about the particular occasion each had been taken.

"This is Mr. Court when he was just about your age, Davy."

"Was that his horsey?" Davy asked, gazing longingly at the little boy in the oversized cowboy hat, a bandana tied at his throat.

"It's a donkey, Davy." Rebecca leaned over Ada's shoulder. "See his big, pointy ears?"

"Oh, yeah. I forget. Was the donkey Mr. Court's?"

Ada shook her head. "Neither was the hat or the bandana. A photographer came with his camera and a donkey and took Mr. Court's picture." She turned the page. "There he is with his daddy playing catch."

"Where is his mommy?"

"She's taking the picture."

"Where is she now?"

Ada smoothed Davy's hair. "She's in heaven with his daddy."

"Oh. No wonder he's kinda mean sometimes. I'd be mean, too, if you went with Daddy and left me." Davy grabbed his mother's hand.

"I have no intention of going to heaven for a long time, Darling."

Davy perused one page and then the next, with a running dialogue from Ada: Mr. Court as a boy riding his bike, Mr. Court in his football uniform, holding a tennis trophy, Mr. Court at Christmas—with his family—with his friends.

"Look, Mommy—there's Pastor Jack."

"So it is." He was taller than Courtney Fielding and just as appealing as he was now.

An article from the high school paper pasted in the album showed the picture of a lean, broad shouldered, grinning lad flexing his muscles. The caption: "Court Fielding wins coveted award: Best Body in Senior Class."

Rebecca smiled. How could she help it? And yet, at the same time, looking at the cheeky boy Courtney Fielding once was made her suddenly very sad.

Davy turned the page. "Who's that?" He pointed at an old lady in a shawl sitting in a wheelchair.

"That's Mr. Court's grandmother," Ada said.

Davy studied the photograph, looked up at Ada and then back again at the picture. "She's as old as you, Ada."

Ada cackled.

"She's in that chair with wheels like Mr. Court's," he observed. "Remember when Mr. Court gave me a ride in his ch—oops." He threw his hand over his mouth. "I wasn't s'posed to tell you, Mommy. Mr. Court made me promise." His eyes were round with chagrin. "Promise you won't tell him I told," he whispered. "Promise."

Rebecca frowned. "I promise. But, Davy, you know you can tell me anything—"

"And there's Mr. Court with his sister, Daisy," Ada inserted, pointing at the next photograph.

If Ada thought Rebecca wasn't smart enough to see through her attempt to change the subject, she had another think coming. Rebecca was about to say so when she thought better of it. What good would it do? The headstrong old lady would do what she pleased anyway. Nevertheless it was irritating when Rebecca herself had made such a concerted effort to keep a sharp eye on Davy so he wouldn't bother the man. Then to find that Ada was instigating just the opposite.

Davy flipped through more pages of the album. "Look. A soldier. We saw lots a soldiers, Mommy—'member?"

Rebecca nodded.

"Don't you know who that is?" Ada asked. "Look close."

"Why, it's Mr. Court," Davy said.

Rebecca gazed down at the photograph of the young soldier standing legs apart, arms akimbo, flirting with the camera. He was tall and broad shouldered, his cap set at a jaunty angle on the back of his head. A shock of dark hair fell across his brow.

The rest of the pages in the album were blank. As if a life had ended.

The cord of sadness tightened around Rebecca's heart. Something about this final picture seemed to pull the parts of the young man's existence together. The humor, the joy, the promise. It was all there, in his audacious stance and sunny, untroubled smile. The Courtney Fielding that Ada remembered, and perhaps saw even now, through the forgiving filter of time.

❧

Court had his routine. He read the newspaper, neatly folded beside his plate each morning, as he ate breakfast. After Rebecca cleared the table and was refreshing his final cup of coffee, he would hand her the want ads, the opportunities he thought promising circled with the same pen he used to complete the paper's daily crossword puzzle.

He had given up asking if she'd been successful in her quest for employment. The results thus far were disappointing. On those mornings when she *was* offered an appointment she would appear at the library door, wearing the same simple dress in which she'd arrived, the same straw hat. Her purse in one white-gloved hand, Davy's small hand in the other, she would ask if there was anything he needed before she left.

The sight of her touched even Court's petrified heart.

On those days, except for the faint sound of Ada's radio in the farther reaches, the mansion was disconcertingly quiet. It seemed he had gotten used to the tinkle of Davy's voice and the lyrical music of Rebecca's response.

By now he thought of her as Rebecca. Perhaps it was because that was the way Jack always referred to her. Although he still addressed her as Mrs. Spaneas.

He had to admit, having the child there wasn't as he had anticipated. Aside from an infrequent dash down the hall and an abject apology from his pursuing mother, Rebecca had managed to channel the boy's primitive energies to the garden. His behavior in the house, for the most part in the solarium, was quite civilized for a four year old, it seemed to Court. And Ada's intrusions with the boy—unbeknownst to Rebecca—added a bit of clandestine glee. It was a secret the three of them shared that brought a brief melody to the monotone of his existence.

After dinner, when he retreated back into the library, he took to leaving the door ajar into the solarium. It was there, in the lingering summer twilight, that Rebecca and Davy had their "deep" discussions, and she told him stories about "The Amazing Davy and His Time Machine."

"Tell me about the time I had lunch with Methuselah, Mommy."

"Again?"

"Yes. Start, 'Once upon a time.'"

From behind his desk in the library Court could see Davy snuggled up against Rebecca in the overstuffed chair on the far side of the couch facing the windows. The shadows were long from the west, the room cast in the rosy glow of declining sunlight.

"Once upon a time, four-year-old Davy was given his very own Bible. Since Davy hadn't yet learned to read—"

"He could read his name. And he knew the alphabet and the sounds, and he knew how to count up to a hundred."

Rebecca smiled. "I think I should start over. Young Davy knew how to count to a hundred. He could identify all the letters in the alphabet, and he knew their sounds. And he could read his name wherever he saw it. So when he got his very own Bible as a birthday present, he saw his name in it. Right then and there, he decided he would learn to read so that he could read the whole Bible from the very beginning to the very end, and he asked his mommy to teach him. And so his mommy and Davy sat down, and they began with the first chapter. That chapter was called"—Rebecca looked down.

"The Book of Genesis." Davy articulated each syllable. "And they read the whole chapter."

"That's right," Rebecca continued. "But that night, as Davy was about to fall asleep, a very strange thing happened—"

Davy interrupted. "In through the window—right through the glass—flew a ball. The ball had two big purple eyes that blinked. It had a green pointy nose and big yellow lips with teeth made out of peppermint candy."

"I don't remember that part," Rebecca said.

"I just made it up—and the ball had big, huge purple wings, bigger than the whole house." Davy spread his arms wide.

"How could it come through the window if its wings were bigger than the whole house?"

"It's imagination, Mommy. Now it's your turn—oh, almost forgot. It had a big sign that said, 'THE AMAZING DAVY'S TIME MACHINE.'"

"That's important," Rebecca said. "The big yellow lips smiled at Davy, and out whooshed a deep voice saying, 'Methuselah has invited you to lunch. Hop in!'"

Court watched with amused interest as Davy filled in the blanks of Rebecca's telling how the machine whisked Davy back into biblical times, how polite and mannerly Davy was, "the way his mommy had taught him." She described what the ancient patriarch wore and how he offered to give Davy a tour of his house.

"When it was time for lunch," Rebecca continued, "Davy didn't ask beforehand what they were going to eat, as some children do."

"My friend, Teddy, used to do that," Davy interjected.

"That's because Teddy didn't know any better. But what did Davy do?"

"Davy said, 'Can I help you set the table?'"

"And Methuselah said—"

"The table already is set."

Rebecca continued. "On the table Davy saw bowls of figs and nuts and chunks of barbequed meat but no forks. 'Where are the forks?' Davy asked Methuselah. And Methuselah said—"

"*WHAT* ARE FORKS?" Davy inserted in a big voice.

"So," Rebecca continued, "Davy took a stick and drew a picture of a fork on the floor."

"He could do that because the floor was made of sand," Davy said.

"That's right. And when Methuselah saw what a fork looked like, he said, 'Well, I guess a person is never too old to learn. But I think I prefer to use my fingers. There are fewer dishes to wash.'"

With that Davy laughed and hugged his mother as if it was the first time this story had been told.

"Now," Davy said, settling back, "tell me the one about—"

"Oh, no, you don't. It's bedtime, my lad." She caught him to her and plopped him on his feet. "How about a little warm milk?"

Court watched them disappear through the kitchen door.

What a great children's book these stories would make! At four, Davy already knew what it was like to live in Bible times. He had been there, in his Amazing Time Machine. Or was it Amazing Davy. Court shrugged. *Either way.*

He looked down at the desk in front of him. To his surprise he saw that while he'd been listening he'd been absently sketching the scenes as Rebecca described them. Davy and Rebecca in the overstuffed chair. Rebecca.

A chill went through him. He hadn't laid pencil to paper since he'd been carried on a stretcher to the base hospital. Nor had he entered his art studio in the year and a half since he'd come home. What once had been as natural to him as breathing, his art, the expression of his heart that gave his life meaning, now seemed frivolous. Worse! With all the pain and suffering in the world, it seemed an indulgence.

Then why, suddenly, without intention, without conscious thought, had he picked up that pencil? He looked down at the scattered sheets. Why, indeed?

Since that first Sunday when he'd watched Rebecca and Jack from behind the drawn drapes of the library, he'd found himself glancing out the window to catch a glimpse of her as she cut flowers in the garden or played with Davy on the north lawn. He anticipated her smile each morning and felt a twinge of disappointment in the evening after she'd paused outside the library door before going to bed. "Is there anything more you need? Then good night, Mr. Fielding." She treated him with the reserved courtesy with which one treats one's employer.

But he, fool that he was, wanted more.

Why would he even entertain the possibility that she would look twice at him? A cripple, who provided little more than a bad disposition and a place for her and her son to lay their heads at night. Until they found another one.

He cringed in embarrassment at his nerve even to harbor such a dream.

Until she came, he had been able to insulate himself, sublimate those desires until they ceased to exist—or so he'd thought. Then she'd showed up and destroyed his armor of protection as thoroughly as she had the antique figurine on that first Sunday.

The solarium was silent, the library so still he could imagine he heard his own heart beating.

He would miss the fresh roses on the dining room table. The lovingly tended plants in the solarium. The birdsong and fresh air floating through the now wide-open windows. He couldn't deny it. When they were gone, he would miss the muted laughter drifting from the kitchen that accompanied his morning cup of coffee. Their voices. Her voice.

He heard her step on the tiled solarium floor.

ten

Rebecca's heels clicked across the tiled floor of the solarium. It was such a lovely room with its walls of glass that brought the garden in during the day and the heavens in at night. Certainly more cheerful than the housekeeper's quarters where she'd just tucked Davy into bed. So far Mr. Courtney Fielding hadn't objected to the time she and Davy spent there in the evenings. He probably hadn't even noticed. He was like a mole, holed up in that library of his.

She paused to pick a dead leaf from the schefflera on the table behind the couch.

If she'd known she was going to be here this long, she'd have made an attempt to resuscitate those drab rooms of the housekeeper's quarters the way she'd resuscitated these plants.

It had been three weeks. It didn't seem possible. The thought made her nervous. How much longer would Mr. Fielding's hospitality hold out? It wasn't as if she hadn't tried to get another job. Even Jack was having trouble, and he had connections. Two for the price of one might be an advantage at the market, but certainly not when it came to housekeepers.

She tried to remind herself that the Lord did things in His own time and that someday she would understand why she must endure yet another disappointment. But she still got disheartened. When the sun fell, her courage appeared to also. She sighed. It always seemed harder at night.

The door to the library was ajar. She could see Courtney Fielding behind the desk, his dark head bent over a sheath of papers. At her knock he scooped them into a drawer.

"Is there anything else you need, Mr. Fielding, before I—"

"Come in, Mrs. Spaneas."

Well, that was a surprise. She and Davy hadn't been invited into the library since the second day after they'd arrived. Why now? Well, at least she was getting more than a grunt and a grudging "No, thank you " that she usually got from him. Braving the man each evening was never the perfect end to a day.

"Come in," he repeated.

Hesitantly Rebecca entered.

"Sit down."

Oh, oh. Her heart accelerated with apprehension. What message of doom was he about to deliver that she needed to sit down?

"How are things going?" he asked. "Any leads with your job search?"

She shook her head. The beginning pangs of panic welled up inside her. She could feel it. The ax was finally about to fall.

Courtney Fielding scratched his jaw. "Jack's coming over tomorrow afternoon. Said he may have a job possibility for you."

"He did? That's wonderful." Rebecca sagged with relief.

"Don't sound too eager, or I'll think you don't like it here."

This was a new tack. The man was evidencing some wit. "Would you like Jack to stay to dinner?" she asked.

"I hadn't thought of that. Sure. Thanks." He paused. "I told him I'd give you a good reference."

"I appreciate that." Rebecca fidgeted beneath his quiet scrutiny and smiled nervously. "I hope your good reference extends to Davy as well."

"Of course."

"But not too good, or one might think you wanted to get rid of us."

"Couldn't be further from the truth." He said it with a smile and what for an instant almost seemed a touch of regret.

But it was so fleeting Rebecca decided it must be her imagination—or wishful thinking.

It hadn't taken her long to get used to this lovely place. She would miss it. She looked up at him through lowered lashes. He hadn't turned out to be nearly as disagreeable as she'd originally expected. Not that he was Mr. Charm. Not by a long shot. But he hadn't been demanding either, and he'd left them alone. And he'd been reasonably appreciative of her efforts—especially those in the kitchen.

"Well, then, if that's all"—she began to rise—"I'll say good night."

"I enjoyed your story this evening." He crossed his arms and leaned back.

She dropped to the edge of the chair. "I am so sorry. I had no idea you could hear us, or I wouldn't—I wish you had said something."

"If it had bothered me, I would have." He smiled. "As a matter of fact I've rather looked forward to my bedtime stories."

"You've been eavesdropping."

"I guess it's the kid in me." He turned more serious. "They're very good. You should write them down."

She looked at him askance.

"I mean it. If you could write them as well as you tell them, I think they'd make a good series of children's books."

She studied him silently for a moment. "Well, I guess you found me out."

"What do you mean?"

She sat back in her chair. "That's always been my dream. I have notebooks filled with ideas and stories for children. Ever since I was a child myself. My major in college was home economics, but I took a lot of writing classes." She smiled. "What a life I had planned—wife,

mother, children's book author. And then the war came."
She glanced away. They'd both had their share of suffering
in the war. "Of course when my husband was killed,
everything changed."

She lifted her eyes. The gaze that met hers was dark and
intense, as if he were looking inside her, seeing her thoughts.
Intuiting on a primitive level that makes words redundant.

Rebecca squirmed uneasily and looked away. "Well, obviously, with a son to raise I've had to choose a more practical
means of support."

The room was silent, broken only by the ticking of the
clock on the mantel.

Finally he said quietly, "Don't give up your dreams, Mrs.
Spaneas." His voice was pensive, his eyes focused on some
inner place, almost as if he were speaking to himself. "If
you don't have your dreams, there's not much point in living, is there?" Then he shrugged, as if in his case the words
didn't apply.

🙣

Court hadn't been able to sleep, but not for the usual reasons.
This time it was Rebecca. He couldn't get her out of his mind
or their conversation the night before.

It was a little after eight in the morning, and already the
breeze blowing through the open dining room window hung
heavy with heat and the scent from the honeysuckle that
crept around the columns of the veranda.

He pushed aside his empty coffee cup.

"Don't give up your dream," he had said. Of all people to give
others advice. He had his nerve. Obviously he embraced the
adage his grandmother had lived by: "Do as I say, not as I do."

When he'd told Rebecca that Jack was following up on an
employment possibility, he could see her excitement. Even
before knowing what it entailed. Apparently anything was
better than being here.

Who could blame her?

As he picked up the crossword puzzle, he heard the whoosh of the swinging door from the butler's pantry. He looked up, anticipating Rebecca's face. Instead Davy inched into the dining room.

For a moment he contemplated Court in silence.

"What's on your mind, Davy?"

"Why do you eat by yourself, Mr. Court?"

"I prefer to."

"Why?"

"I like peace and quiet so I can do the crossword puzzle."

"You don't do the crossword puzzle when you eat dinner. You eat by yourself then."

"That's true."

"If you want to, you can eat with me and Mommy in the kitchen. We don't mind." Davy's round brown eyes bespoke his sincerity.

"Thank you, Davy, but I don't think so."

"We could talk."

"I come to eat, not talk."

"Me and Mommy eat *and* talk. But I don't talk with my mouth full. We can talk about when you were a boy like me and had your picture taken on a donkey and played ball with your daddy. And when you were a soldier. I saw a picture of when you were a soldier in Ada's album, and you weren't sitting down. Ada says you're very brave."

Court wiped his mouth and laid his napkin beside his plate. "Ada's prejudiced."

"What's preja—preja—"

"She thinks better of me than I deserve."

"Ada says you draw pretty pictures."

"Not anymore."

"Ada says to ask you if I can see your pictures."

"I think I'm going to have to give Ada more work to do."

"Why?"

"So she won't have so much time to talk. Take this to your mother, please." Court handed Davy the want-ad section of the newspaper and backed away from the table. He wheeled his chair around and with a heaving thrust pushed himself through the door just as Rebecca rounded the corner.

Too late!

She threw out her hands and tumbled into him, clutching his shoulders and landing in his lap.

Instinctively Court caught her.

The wheelchair tilted to the side, rocked back, then steadied.

Stunned, they stared at each other, their faces close enough to kiss.

Without moving, Court murmured, "Are you okay?"

Rebecca nodded.

He could feel the grip of her fingers grasping his shoulders and the firmness of her waist beneath his hands. He could see the tiny pale freckles across the bridge of her nose. She had the faint smell of cinnamon.

"I'm so sorry," she whispered. "I didn't see—I was looking for—"

As she spoke, warm plumes of breath exploded softly against his lips.

Their gazes held.

Davy ran up beside them. "Are you going to give Mommy a ride in your chair like you did me?"

Court looked at him then threw back his head and laughed. "Why not?" Before Rebecca could react he was whizzing down the hall with her on his lap. Into the solarium, around the couch and back, with Rebecca desperately clinging to his shoulders and Davy running beside them shouting, "Faster! Faster!"

"Stop!" she cried. "Stop!"

But her protestations fell on deaf ears as Court spun

around the dining room table, at last grinding to a sudden halt that threw her so hard against him that the chair tilted again, threatening to tip them both onto the polished oak floor.

Rebecca scrambled off his lap. "Really, Mr. Fielding. Really." Agitated, she shook her head, smoothed her dress and tucked her hair back into its French knot.

But he could see by the look in her large brown eyes and the upturned twist to the corners of her lips that she wasn't as angry as she was making out.

Davy jumped up and down clapping his hands and laughing.

"You're a bad influence, Davy," Court said and wheeled down the hall and into the library, shutting the door behind him.

What had possessed him?

❧

Rebecca stared after him. She felt breathless and disoriented from the dizzying ride—and from the lemony scent of his aftershave. She tingled where his hands had circled her waist and felt weak remembering his azure eyes darkening to indigo as they stared into hers.

What possessed her?

She could only imagine.

eleven

The doorbell rang while Davy—with Rebecca's oversight—was setting the dining room table.

He dropped a fork haphazardly on the place mat and ran toward the door. "It's Pastor Jack."

Rebecca grabbed the back of his shirt. "Oh, no, you don't."

"Why not?"

"This is Mr. Court's house. We must do things properly."

"Mr. Court doesn't care."

"I wouldn't be so sure about that. Besides, I care. You stay right where you are. You'll have plenty of chance to visit with Pastor Jack in good time." She strode into the entry, leaving a pouting Davy behind the closed dining room door.

Jack stepped inside the house. "Rebecca, you look wonderful." He gave her an admiring glance and handed her an elegantly wrapped box.

She looked down at the box of chocolates and returned his smile. "Of course you know you've discovered the way to my heart."

"That was my intention." He grinned.

Courtney Fielding wheeled in, frowning. "I hope I'm not interrupting."

"Well. . ." Jack let an eloquent pause elapse. "I guess you're entitled. It's your house." He smiled and extended his hand. "How are you doing, old man?"

"I'm fine. So are you, I'd say."

"It's the company."

"Clearly not mine." Courtney Fielding glanced at Rebecca. Like a jealous little boy, she thought.

"Thanks for inviting me to dinner," Jack said.

"It was her idea." Courtney Fielding shrugged.

"Well, then, thank you, Rebecca."

Rebecca laughed. "I doubt you suffer much from lack of invitations. An eligible young minister must be constant grist for the church mothers' marriage mill."

"Be assured, I'm not easily swayed by chicken and dumplings or tuna fish casseroles," Jack said, assuming a staunch expression.

"How about roast beef and Yorkshire pudding?"

"That I could be swayed by." He looked around. "Where's the butler?"

"I'm in here." The small muffled voice came from behind the dining room door. It opened a crack. "I'm setting the table."

Jack strode through it. "Hi, Davy, lad." He crouched down and gave the boy a bear hug.

Standing by the front door, Rebecca glanced toward her employer.

He was hunched in his wheelchair, his elbows on the arm-rests. Head lowered, he gazed at the easy, affectionate exchange between Jack and Davy. Rebecca saw again his sadness, regret, sense of isolation. She knew she witnessed what she was not meant to see, what no one was meant to see, and felt an almost overwhelming urge to go to him, wrap her arms around him as she would a troubled child and give him comfort.

He looked up and caught her watching. At once, the mask of his defenses fell into place. His eyes hardened. Abruptly he pushed his chair forward, following his friend into the dining room.

As Rebecca followed, she saw Davy pointing out his mastery of table setting to Jack. "See—the big fork goes on this side, and the little one goes here, next to it."

"I see only two places, Davy," Jack said.

"Me and Mommy eat in the kitchen." He glanced at Courtney Fielding without rancor. "Mr. Court eats alone—so he don't have to talk and he can do his crossword puzzles."

Jack looked down at his friend and shook his head.

Courtney Fielding averted his eyes.

"Well, Davy," Jack said, "tonight everyone's welcome at the table."

Rebecca touched Davy's shoulder. "You and Mr. Fielding have things to discuss, Jack. Besides, Davy and I are perfectly happy—"

"As a matter of fact," Jack interrupted, "what we have to discuss affects you and Davy. Isn't that so, Court?"

Rebecca demurred. "Please, I'd really rather not."

"Just set two more places, Mrs. Spaneas," Courtney Fielding said impatiently, whipping his chair up to the table.

❧

Rebecca sat at the table on Courtney Fielding's left, across from Jack, with Davy beside her.

Jack wiped his mouth with his linen napkin. "Delicious roast beef, Rebecca. And that Yorkshire pudding"—he brought his fingers to his pursed lips—"perfection!"

Rebecca preened as the compliments went on.

"The mashed potatoes, not a lump. And the fresh green peas. The fresh green peas popped with every bite."

Courtney Fielding lifted his glass and took a drink of water. No accolades from that quarter.

"Do you eat like this all the time?" the minister asked him.

His friend nodded. He didn't look at Rebecca. "Mrs. Spaneas is an excellent cook. Excellent."

A compliment?

"Her bread pudding is delicious, but wait until you taste her chocolate cake."

She could hardly believe her ears.

"Can I be 'scused?" Davy asked. "I help Mommy clear the

forks and spoons," he told the pastor.

"Good show." Jack began to rise. "Let me help, too."

Rebecca shook her head. "No, please, Davy and I can handle it. You keep Mr. Fielding company."

When the dishes were cleared, Rebecca carried in a silver tray on which there were three cups of coffee, a glass of milk and a triple-layer German chocolate cake on an elegant cut-glass cake plate. Davy followed with the spoons and forks. She sliced the cake with a sterling silver cake knife, placing the wedges gently on antique Limóge dessert plates, all but Davy's, which she served on serviceable pottery from the kitchen.

The men consumed the moist morsels without conversation, their silence a compliment in itself.

When Courtney Fielding had finished, he looked over at Davy's plate and reached a menacing fork toward the pile of rich, dark frosting Davy had scraped from his piece. "Oh, you don't like frosting. Then you won't mind if I help myself."

Davy warded off the threatening implement with his small hand. "Oh, no, Mr. Court, frosting's my favorite. That's why I save it 'til last. I'd give you some, but you might get my germites."

"Your what?"

"My germites. You know."

"Oh, yes." Courtney Fielding licked a crumb of chocolate from the corner of his mouth and murmured aside to Jack. "I would probably benefit from some of his germites."

"Wouldn't we all?" Jack laughed and turned to Davy. "I can see you're a big help to your mother, setting the table and helping her clear."

"Indeed he is." Rebecca smiled fondly at her son.

Davy gave the minister a toothy chocolate smile. "I'm a big help to Ada, too." He swallowed a swig of milk. "I help Ada just like you used to, Mr. Court."

"Is that so?"

Davy nodded. "I help her polish the table and shine the silver. And I carry her dust rag. But she won't let me carry the heavy stuff." He took another bite of cake.

Rebecca straightened. "Ada can use all the help she can get, poor dear."

At last. Davy had given Rebecca the opportunity she'd been waiting for. "I've been meaning to talk to you about Ada."

Courtney Fielding interrupted. "May I have a bit more of that cake?"

Clearly Ada was not a topic of vital interest to him. Rebecca accepted his plate and cut him another piece of cake. "She has terribly painful arthritis. Seeing her lug all her cleaning supplies up and down the stairs is hard to watch." She handed back the plate. "Perhaps you hadn't noticed."

"Yes. Poor old thing. I told her she should use the elevator." He took a generous bite of cake.

"Using the elevator is supposed to make her job easier? I'm sorry, Mr. Fielding. Ada is still doing far more than what should be expected of a woman her age. I've tried to help her, but she won't hear of it."

"She lets Davy help her," Courtney Fielding reminded her.

"Davy's a wonderful help"—Rebecca patted her son's arm—"but he's only four." She gave her employer an oblique look. "How long has Ada been working for your family, Mr. Fielding?" She knew the answer but wanted to hear him admit it.

He wiped his mouth. "Let's see. Sixty years, at least. Talk about an old family retainer. She's well past retirement age, that's for sure." He forked another bite into his mouth.

Had the man no shame? No compassion?

She glanced at Jack, but he looked as bland as his friend.

The anger she had felt before—and managed to suppress—

about Ada's shabby treatment suddenly struck her like a fist in her stomach. The inequity of it. It was positively indecent the way the poor beleaguered thing was being treated. "I'm sorry, Mr. Fielding, but in all conscience I must speak out."

Courtney Fielding, as well as the pastor, looked up, surprised.

"I'm sure you haven't noticed how frail Ada is or how hard she works. This job is shortening her life. She never complains, so you probably don't realize how severe her medical problems are."

"Believe me, Mrs. Spaneas—I'm fully aware of Ada's medical history." Courtney Fielding pushed back his empty plate and glanced at Jack.

"If you are, then how can you possibly continue to expect so much of her?"

"It's her choice."

Rebecca was appalled. "You have to be kidding." Jack and Davy had become peripheral. Courtney Fielding was her target. Casting caution to the winds, Rebecca made no effort to hide her contempt. "I know all about Ada's debt to you. She confided that she would never be able to pay you back, even if she worked the rest of her life." Rebecca allowed her eyes to make a slow scan of the elegantly appointed table. "Surely you can afford to be generous and forgive her debt. Besides, it's not legal to keep indentured servants—especially ones that are eighty years old."

"Eighty-two," Courtney Fielding corrected.

It was then Rebecca noticed that Jack's shoulders were shaking with suppressed laughter. He held up his hand and caught his breath. "You're talking about the most stubborn old dear ever born."

Tears came into Rebecca's eyes. She was too incensed to consider the ramifications of her outburst and blundered on. "I can believe Mr. Fielding's insensitivity, but you, Jack—I'm shocked."

"Wait a minute, Rebecca. There are two sides to this story." Jack put his hand on Courtney Fielding's arm.

Rebecca was appalled. "How can you defend him?"

"I know how it may look to you. But this man whom you are maligning—my best buddy—not only paid for the 'old dear's' two hip operations, but he also paid her hospital expenses when she had her stroke, he paid for her eye operation, and he continues to pay for all her medication. He begged Ada to retire. Didn't you, Court?"

Courtney Fielding nodded.

"Of course she refused," Jack said, "being the stubborn, proud old lady that she is. So he pays her pension anyway—"

"You don't need to go into the details, Jack," Courtney Fielding said.

"—which is the full amount of her salary—which she refuses to take unless she works for it—despite the fact that she can hardly see."

"Mrs. Spaneas has heard enough." It was obvious Courtney Fielding was getting embarrassed and annoyed.

"I'm almost finished." Jack was not to be deterred. "Once a month Court hires a cleaning crew, on Ada's day off so her feelings won't be hurt."

"What's a cleaning crew?" Davy asked.

Chagrined, Jack focused on Davy. "It's a secret for now, Davy," he said, obviously distressed that he had not been more circumspect in the presence of the small boy whose large brown eyes and sharp ears had taken it all in. Even though he might not have understood it.

Rebecca felt like a deflated balloon. She'd just given her employer, and her minister, a full dose of her worst fault, jumping to conclusions. The nerve of her! If there were a hole big enough, she would have crawled into it. On second thought she was in a hole—one she had dug with her own big mouth. She was in it, with no way to crawl out.

And to make matters worse she had done it all in front of her precious son.

She didn't know what to say. "I am so sorry. I am so embarrassed. I don't know. If what Pastor Jack says is true—"

"Would a preacher lie?" Jack interjected.

"Clearly you have been more than generous and kind. . . ." Her words petered out as she looked up at Courtney Fielding. Rather than anger, she saw amusement reflected in his electric blue eyes.

"What can I tell you?" He shrugged. "I'm a saint."

"Well, I wouldn't go that far." Jack gave him a playful punch. He turned back to Rebecca, his face serious. "Ada's not the only one Court takes care of—"

"And my friend here has a big mouth." Courtney Fielding gave him a warning look and abruptly changed the subject. "Now might be a good time to tell Rebecca about that possibility regarding future employment."

twelve

Rebecca leaned over and lifted her son out of his chair. "We have grown-up things to talk about now, Davy. You go upstairs and put on your jammies and brush your teeth."

"I wanna stay with Mr. Court and Pastor Jack." Davy thrust out his lower lip.

"You can come back down when you're finished."

"You promise?"

Rebecca nodded. "Now git." Facing him toward the door, she gave his backside a soft swat. "And brush your teeth well, or you'll have to go back up and do them again."

When he was gone, she said, "Children are resilient, but they get attached. To things. . .to people." She dropped her gaze. She'd noticed that Davy had formed just such an attachment to Courtney Fielding, who treated him with acceptance and warmth, although she knew those moments were not the ones the man intended her to see. "I don't want him to worry about moving away until the time comes." She raised her eyes. "Now tell me about this opportunity, Jack."

The minister smiled. "It's amazing, the mysterious ways God works. He manages to put us in the right spot at exactly the right moment."

"Or the wrong spot at the wrong moment." Courtney Fielding pushed his wheelchair back from the table and crossed his arms. "We don't need a sermon, Jack. Get on with it."

His friend gave him a brief, empathetic glance and turned back to Rebecca. "Yesterday I called the preacher at the Pasadena Baptist Church and told him about you. Perfect timing! He'd just come back from visiting one of his congregation at the hospital—an independent, elderly lady in her eighties, living alone—"

"Sounds like somebody we know," Courtney Fielding mumbled.

"—who'd broken her hip."

"That's especially serious with an older person," Rebecca murmured.

"It looks like she'll be all right. But the doctor says that if she's going to continue to live at home, she has to have full-time help."

"How soon will that be?" Courtney Fielding asked.

"Obviously not soon enough to suit you, Mr. Fielding," Rebecca murmured, lifting her chin a mite.

"Don't be defensive, Mrs. Spaneas," he said. "That's not what I was inferring."

Jack pushed back his plate and put his elbows on the table. "If you're in a hurry, that's a problem. She'll be in the convalescent hospital recuperating for at least two months. Whoever she hires won't begin work until about the middle of September."

Rebecca glanced at Courtney Fielding. "That's an awfully long time to wait."

"But you'd probably have a good chance of getting the job," he observed. "I doubt she's started interviewing yet."

"She just broke her hip day before yesterday," his guest remarked.

"Did you tell your friend I had a child?" Rebecca asked.

Jack nodded. "He said he was pretty sure that wouldn't be a problem. Apparently she's a retired schoolteacher. Loves children. Still teaches Sunday school, in fact. Or did, until this happened. And she has a guest house, so whoever she hires will have a place of their own."

"It sounds too good to be true," Rebecca said.

"Don't get your hopes up until you meet her," Court said. "Some old people are very demanding and difficult."

Both Rebecca and Jack turned their eyes on him.

"All right," he muttered. "So you don't have to be old to be difficult. I just mean"—his voice lowered, as if the words were hard to come by—"I just mean you shouldn't rush into anything. You don't want to make a mistake. . .for Davy's sake. Like you said, kids form attachments. You wouldn't want to have to uproot him again."

Jack steepled his fingers. "There is a solution."

"What's that?"

"Don't uproot him in the first place."

"That's already been settled," Courtney Fielding said sharply.

Jack's gaze met Rebecca's.

"Believe me." Her voice was firm. "Mr. Fielding and I are of like mind. I am as determined as he that I find other employment."

Jack lowered his hands to his knees. "In that case, if the time element doesn't create a problem"—he looked at Rebecca and at Court, who shrugged—"then I'll set up an appointment as soon as possible for you to meet her."

"That would be wonderful," Rebecca said.

"You do drive, don't you?"

"Yes." She frowned. "But I don't have a California driver's license."

"I can take you to get one," Jack said.

Courtney Fielding raked back that shock of hair. "Well, that solves a problem for me."

"What's that?" Jack asked.

"Ada's grandson, Paul, who takes me to therapy, is changing to the day shift next month. He can still drop me off."

"And I can bring you home," Rebecca said brightly.

Courtney Fielding nodded. "You can drive the convertible."

"What happens when Rebecca leaves?" Jack picked an imaginary piece of lint from his sleeve.

They both shot him a steely look.

He shrugged. "Just a thought."

"I'm very grateful to you," Rebecca said. "I know you've gone to a lot of trouble."

"I should have more such trouble." Jack's brown eyes held a flicker of warmth that went beyond pastoral duty.

At that moment Davy padded back into the dining room wearing his Doctor Denton pajamas with the feet in them. "I brushed my teeth real good." He cracked a showy smile all around.

Rebecca inspected. "Good for you, Sweetie." She rose. "Can I offer anyone more coffee? A little more cake?"

Jack patted his stomach. "You were right, Court. That chocolate cake was outstanding. But I don't have an ounce of room left."

"I'll give you some to take home—if it's all right with Mr. Fielding."

"By all means."

"Will you give me a ride, Mr. Court?" Without waiting for an answer, Davy had jumped into the man's lap.

"Where are your manners?" Chagrined, Rebecca reached toward him, only to have her hand moved aside.

"Davy and I understand each other. Don't we, Son?" Courtney Fielding said.

Davy snuggled up against him. "Let's go fast, like you did when Mommy was in your lap."

Rebecca almost dropped the plate she had lifted. Maybe Jack hadn't heard. The expression on his face told her otherwise. She gave an embarrassed laugh. "It's not what it seems. Mr. Fielding ran into me with that machine of his, and I fell—"

"Don't let her kid you. She did it on purpose." Courtney Fielding was smirking as he and Davy whizzed out of the dining room.

Rebecca turned to Jack. "Are you going to believe him?"

"I'm willing to reserve judgment until I've heard your side of the story."

"Men!"

With Jack on her heels and her hands full of plates, Rebecca stamped across the dining room, kicked the door to the butler's pantry open and strode through it. It swung back with such force that, had the pastor not been agile, it would have wiped out the stack of dishes he was balancing.

❧

After a considerable number of minutes whizzing through the downstairs of the Fielding mansion while Rebecca, with Jack's assistance, cleaned up after dinner, Court and Davy settled themselves at the library desk with paper and pencil.

While Davy drew, Court was distracted by thoughts of Rebecca and Jack in the kitchen. He couldn't believe it took that long to clean up a few measly dishes. He wondered what they were talking about and for a moment entertained the idea that he and Davy might join them. But pride intervened.

A few minutes later Davy looked up as Rebecca and Jack entered. "Look, Mommy—I'm a artist." He held up a sheet of paper. "Mr. Court teached me how to draw a bunny."

"He's a very good artist," Court said.

"Why, that's excellent," Rebecca said. "Look at Davy's bunny, Pastor Jack."

"I'd certainly recognize it as a bunny," Jack said. "Very good, Davy."

Court adjusted the boy in his lap. "There are books and toys in the attic that Daisy and I played with when we were children. Tomorrow ask Ada if she can show you where they are. There's no reason why Davy can't enjoy them."

"Thank you, Mr. Fielding. That's generous of you," Rebecca said.

"We'll see," he mumbled. Being thought generous was not the role he wanted. "For all I know, by now the mice might have gotten them."

"Mice?" Davy's head popped up from his work. "Teach me to draw a mice, Mr. Court."

"The magic word?" Rebecca reminded her son.

"Please."

"And that's your last picture for tonight, Davy. You know it's way past your bedtime," she said.

Davy extended the moment as long as he could. Finally he laid down the pencil. "This one's for you, Mr. Court." He handed Court the picture he'd just finished.

"Thanks, Davy."

"We'll hang it tomorrow," Davy said, jumping off his lap. He ran over to his mother with the rest of his stash. "Here, Mommy—you can give one to Pastor Jack. The rest are for you to hang up."

"We're going to have quite a gallery," she said, glancing at Court. "Now say good night to Pastor Jack and Mr. Court."

Davy bestowed the requisite squeeze on Jack then ran over and, leaping again into Court's lap, gave him a hearty bear hug.

"Okay, okay, Davy." Court tried to disengage him. But Davy persevered, adding an extended nose-brushing Eskimo kiss for good measure. Court was even more embarrassed by the conspicuous display when he saw the look of surprise reflected on the faces of Jack and Rebecca.

Davy giggled and wouldn't let go until Rebecca had forcibly removed him.

"I think it's time we said good night," she said, struggling with the squirming child. "Thank you for including us."

"Thank you," Jack said, "for your charming company and that delicious dinner."

"Yes, very good," Court echoed.

"Stop wiggling, Davy." Over her son's shoulder Rebecca gave Jack a smile that lit the far corners of the room.

Lucky Jack.

"Don't forget to take your cake," she said.

"No chance."

She turned her smile on Court. "Don't worry, Mr. Fielding—there's plenty left. I wouldn't forget you."

If only that were true.

Both Court and Jack sat mute, listening to the diminishing murmur of Rebecca's and Davy's voices until the house fell silent.

"She's quite a woman," Jack murmured, dropping into the chair in front of the desk.

"Isn't she?"

"Mmm."

"I don't like that look," Court said.

"What look is that?"

"The pastoral counseling look."

"Sorry. I can't help it." Jack smiled. "That's just me. It's endemic to my personality."

"You forget. I knew your personality before you assumed the mantle of the minister."

"You're the one responsible, remember?"

"That was a long time ago. A lot of water has gone under the bridge since then."

"That may be," Jack said quietly, "but no amount is enough to wash away my prayers for you."

Court gave him a hard look. "Don't waste them."

"We'll see." Jack tapped his fingers on the arm of the

chair. "Have you really considered what it's going to be like here without Rebecca and Davy?"

"I don't think about it."

"Oh, I think you do. You may try not to, but you do. It's on your face when you look at that boy—when you look at her."

"I got along fine before they came. I'll get along fine when they're gone." He gave his friend an oblique look. "If you think she's so great, why don't *you* hire her?"

"I would, but I'm afraid folks might talk." Jack laughed.

It seemed a hollow laugh to Court and held scant humor. He saw in his friend's eyes the thoughts he accused Court of having.

Jack was beginning to have feelings for Rebecca, too.

Court felt an emptiness in the pit of his stomach. He loved this man like a brother, ever since they were boys. In Court's darkest days Jack had stood by him. If more befell him, Jack would still be there. But as Court gazed at his friend another feeling threatened. An aching, destructive feeling.

Envy!

No, it was worse, more complicated than envy. Anger and jealousy made the brew even more volatile. Anger at what was denied him and jealousy for what Jack had— what his vibrant friend was destined to have if he chose.

Court lowered his eyes to his clenched hands on the desk in front of him. If only he could believe there was a God. He had once. Once he could have prayed these feelings away. But experience had taught him otherwise. No longer could he be seduced by the promises of love and mercy and forgiveness, as set forth in the Gospels. He'd seen different. He'd lived different.

He willed his face to go blank. "When will you take Rebecca to get her driver's license?" he asked.

"I thought maybe Friday," Jack said. "I could arrange to have her meet the lady then, too. I invited her to lunch, but she said she had to ask you, since it wasn't her day off."

"What about Davy? Did you include him in your invitation?"

Jack grinned. "The two of you seem to get along so splendidly that I thought you might baby-sit." He leaned forward. "Ada will be here. Do you mind?"

thirteen

The dining room was located on the west side of the house and always seemed rather somber in the morning to Rebecca. She placed the glass of orange juice on the table, just so, above the knife, and straightened the napkin, turning as Courtney Fielding wheeled into the room. "Good morning."

"Good morning, Mrs. Spaneas."

"I was just thinking that one day you might like to try your breakfast in the solarium. It's so much more cheerful in the morning." She stepped aside as he rolled to the place she had set for him at the head of the table.

The air was rich with the morning smells of frying bacon and—

"Burned toast!" She dashed from the room, returning a few minutes later with a plate of scrambled eggs, country fries and bacon, which she laid before him.

"Crisp, just the way I like it. There's an art to frying bacon that I wish Neda could master." He broke off a bite and popped it into his mouth. "But she does make a mean toast."

"It's on its way," Rebecca said. "So what about it?"

"About what?"

"The solarium. Would you like to try breakfast in the solarium tomorrow morning?"

"I'll think about it." He took a forkful of scrambled eggs and swallowed thoughtfully. "These are delicious."

Rebecca smiled. "I added a bit of truffle oil I found hidden in the back of the cupboard."

"Delicious. Tell Neda about it. Toast?"

"Sorry." She hurried out of the dining room, returning with a small plate of buttered toast and a crock of fresh strawberry jam.

Since those unpleasant moments when she'd first arrived, Rebecca and Courtney Fielding had gradually settled into an easy, if somewhat reserved, relationship, permitted, perhaps, by the fact that they both knew it was not to be permanent.

"When I visited my grandmother as a kid, we used to take all of our meals in the solarium during the summer." He picked up a triangle of toast and spread it with jam.

Rebecca paused. Usually by now he was buried in the morning paper—or the crossword puzzle. She and Davy had been well schooled not to bother him. But this morning he seemed to want her to stay.

"I wouldn't be displacing you and Davy, would I, if I ate breakfast in the solarium?"

"Oh, no. We take our meals in the kitchen. Besides, even if you were, it's your house."

"Yes." For a moment he paused then lifted his napkin and wiped his mouth.

Rebecca moved toward the pantry door.

"Where are you going?"

"To get you some hot coffee."

"Oh."

As she topped off his second cup, he said, "Jack tells me you're getting your driver's license Friday."

"If it's all right with you."

"I have no objection. He also said you would be interviewing for the position with your potential employer."

"If he can arrange it. Assuming you don't need me back here too early."

"And that you and Jack are planning to go out to lunch."

"Only with your permission."

"You're not a slave, Mrs. Spaneas," he said impatiently. "Jack intimated that I should baby-sit Davy."

She frowned. "He certainly didn't discuss that with me. I assumed we'd take Davy with us." She returned the coffeepot to the silver service on the butler's chest. "I wouldn't hear of you baby-sitting."

"How about Ada?"

"That's different."

"So you wouldn't trust me with your son, but you consider it part of poor old Ada's job description?"

"I didn't say that."

"You didn't have to." By now he had finished his breakfast. He picked up the newspaper, pushed himself back from the table and wheeled toward the entry.

It was frustrating. On the one hand he could be so pleasant, even caring, as he was with Davy. On the other, he would blindside her, try to bait her. As he seemed to be doing now.

Rebecca strode across the room and placed herself between him and the door.

He rolled forward, stopping just short of her toes. "Excuse me."

Barring his way, she thrust her hands on her hips and glared down at him. "I have been here almost a month, Mr. Fielding. I have gone on interviews and errands, and I have always taken Davy with me. I have never even been tempted to impose on Ada. And *certainly* not on you. You made that very clear when I arrived."

"Mommy."

Rebecca turned to see Davy's head poking through the pantry door. "Go back in the kitchen," she said sharply. "I'll be with you in a minute."

She lowered her voice. "And since you used my son as the reason to get rid of me, I hardly think I would be so stupid as to wish to suffer that indignity again." She paused for breath. "Once is definitely enough."

"Calm down, Mrs. Spaneas. I didn't say we wouldn't baby-sit. Don't you think you're overreacting a bit?"

Calm down? Overreacting? He sounded so superior. If he was trying to incite her, he was certainly succeeding. "You—you are impossible!" As quickly as the words were out she was appalled at her gall—to say nothing of her lack of self-control.

The time pressure to find new employment was one she had put on herself. That she would leave was taken for granted from the beginning. But since then, as he had last night, he had only urged her not to make a hasty decision she might later regret. For Davy's sake.

Yes, she imposed the pressure. Rebecca had come to realize that the longer she stayed in this house, the less she wanted to leave it.

She dropped her hands from her hips and lowered her eyes. "Oh, Mr. Fielding, I am so sorry. I had no right—"

"Endure, Mrs. Spaneas. You won't have to put up with my ill humor much longer. I have a feeling you'll get this job on Friday, and then your troubles will be over." Suddenly Rebecca realized how very personal it had become. Her gaze met his again and, for a long moment, held. Was it her imagination, or was that regret flickering in the shadows of Courtney Fielding's sardonic gaze?

"I am so sorry," she repeated softly.

Then the spell was broken. His expression cooled. His mouth tightened; his shoulders squared. He put his hands on the push rims of his chair. "I'm afraid you'll have to move, Mrs. Spaneas, or I might think you want to go for another ride. And how would we explain that to Ada and her grandson, Paul?"

❧

In his bedroom Court faced himself in the full-length mirror and stared belligerently into the brown eyes glaring back at him. His gaze raked over the lips, tightened into an unyielding line, and the shoulders, stiff with tension.

Why was he so mean to her? Intentionally so. Yet even as he knew he often hurt her, he felt helpless to do otherwise, protecting himself, fearful she would get too close.

Even in this he was a coward.

As before, as always, he had failed. She broke through his defenses. He had seen it as her angry gaze softened into understanding. As if she could see into the heart of him.

Why had she come?

Another of God's dirty tricks to torment him, to exact further punishment for living when his comrades had died. Died because he had chosen them, picked them one by one as the strongest and the bravest, and then led them to the slaughter. That all-powerful God who was supposed to protect them—whom he'd counted on to protect them—had stuck His finger down from the clouds and said, "Zap! You're dead!"

But He had missed Court. For that, Court could never forgive Him.

A bold knock on the bedroom door interrupted his angry rumination.

"Mr. Court, it's Paul. If we don't leave now, we'll be late for your therapy appointment."

"Give me a couple of minutes. I'll meet you in the downstairs hall."

Court swung his chair around. Why did he bother? Nothing was going to change.

He ran his hands over his thighs. His legs looked normal enough, felt strong, thanks to the physical therapy three times a week.

He could hear the psychiatrist's voice. "What you have, Lieutenant Fielding, is conversion hysteria brought on by emotional stress. This condition is manifested by physical symptoms such as blindness, inability to speak or, as in your case, paralysis, with no medical evidence to substantiate them. It's not as uncommon as you might think for one who has suffered the extreme trauma that you have," the psychiatrist had said pedantically. "What is unusual is the length of time you have had the symptom."

Nothing had worked; even drug therapy and electroshock therapy had proved unsuccessful. He wondered why he put himself through it. Three times a week for over a year and a half. The physical therapy was exhausting, the mental therapy even more so. At the end of each session he vowed it would be his last. But then, two days later, there he was, at it again.

He pulled open the bedroom door and wheeled into the hall.

What was it that kept him going? What was it that kept that small, pale, flickering flame of hope alive?

fourteen

The last thing Courtney Fielding did as he wheeled out the front door to go to his therapy was to instruct Ada to find the toys in the attic for Davy. Rebecca thought that considerate in view of the unpleasantness at breakfast.

Gazing up from the bottom of the precipitous attic stairs, Rebecca said, "They look almost as steep as the Horns of Negros above Dumaguete in the Philippines. I hate to have you climb them, Ada. I'm sure Davy and I can find the toys Mr. Fielding mentioned."

"Oh, I can make it. I'll just take it slow," Ada said. "It'll be like visiting old friends; it's been so long since I've been up there."

Take it slow, she did. Wheezing all the way, Ada preceded Davy and Rebecca up the stairs, one arduous step after another. With both hands she dragged herself up the banister, planting a foot on the step above then pulling the other to meet it. Halfway up she paused for a breather. "It'll be easier comin' down."

Behind her, Davy clutched the rail and kept up a constant monologue on the anticipated treasures he was soon to discover.

While Rebecca and Davy waited on the narrow steps just below her, Ada removed a ring of keys from her uniform pocket. Methodically she tried each one until finally she found a fit in the tarnished lock. After several rattling tries the key engaged. Ada turned the knob, and the door creaked slowly open to the discordant harmony of its squealing hinges.

The three paused on the threshold peering into the vast dim space. Shrouded with sheets, hulking forms with sharp angles and threatening bulges loomed before them. Stacks of boxes and mysterious bags leaned together or spilled their contents on the littered floor.

"I'm scared," Davy whimpered, huddling closer to Rebecca. He clutched the hem of her skirt. "I don't think there's anything I want in there."

"Courage, Davy." Ada's gnarled hand skimmed the wall just inside the door. "You won't be scared when I find the pesky light switch." Across the room dust motes danced in the narrow fingers of light pushing through the blinds. Ada began to cough. "This place could use a good airing out."

Suddenly a small, suspended bulb in the middle of the room blinked on, not bright, but light enough to turn the once menacing forms into old dressers, nightstands, tables and chairs and the boxes and bags into receptacles for children's books and toys.

The first thing Rebecca did was to make her way through the cluttered room to the windows opposite. She snapped open the shutters and lifted the sashes, letting in the sun and the sweet summer air. The morning haze had burned off, and she leaned out, gazing across the manicured grounds of the Fielding estate and the arroyo beyond, toward the San Gabriels that looked almost close enough to touch. It filled her heart with peace. She would miss it!

"Look, Mommy."

She turned.

Davy stood at attention, his small hand lifted in a smart salute. It emerged from the sleeve of a military jacket bedecked with combat ribbons and medals. It pooled on the floor around him. A lieutenant's military cap slid rakishly over one eye and would have obscured his face completely had it not been for his ear holding it up.

"Mr. Court's uniform," Ada said, moisture glistening in her eyes. "He was so brave."

"Do I look brave, Mommy?"

"Indeed you do, Davy." Rebecca swallowed the lump in her throat. "But maybe for now it would be best to put the uniform back where you got it. This attic is awfully dirty, and you have a lot more investigating to do."

"I bet Mr. Court doesn't mind if I wear it."

Rebecca glanced at Ada. "I'm not so sure about that."

"I know Mr. Court. He wouldn't mind a bit."

Rebecca perused the room then strode to the corner. "With that big uniform on, you wouldn't be able to ride this." She held up a child's tricycle. Though thick with dust the wheel still spun smoothly.

And that wasn't all. In addition to cartons of books there were teddy bears and dolls. And a Lionel train.

"And look, Davy—a whole set of big wood blocks," Rebecca said.

There was a little red wagon, a small child's easel and a table and two chairs just Davy's size. All the whimsical things that most children can only imagine and few possess.

"What's this?" Davy asked, holding up a silver figure with its broken arm upraised.

Rebecca reached down and picked up a similar figure from the box at his feet. That one held a tennis ball aloft. She could see where the racket had once been.

Ada shook her head sadly. "Mr. Court's tennis trophies." She shuffled over to a bookcase against the wall and skimmed the spines. "High school yearbooks," she said, pulling one out and handing it to Rebecca. "His senior year."

As Rebecca thumbed through the pages, she understood why Ada's eyes had grown moist. She had to fight back her own tears.

It was the year Courtney Fielding had graduated. Ada had opened the yearbook to his senior picture. Formal, in coat and tie, his smile broad, his eyes shining with expectation and hope. Without a doubt the handsomest boy on the page. He appeared confident without looking cocky.

She reached up and touched his face and the recalcitrant shock of dark hair that even then refused to be tamed.

As she turned the pages she read the captions beneath the pictures: Court Fielding makes winning touchdown, Court Fielding brings home All-State trophy in tennis, Court Fielding leads team to victory, Court Fielding as the doctor in the senior play, Court Fielding wins art scholarship, Court Fielding, Court Fielding. . . . And then the notes written from his classmates, careless scrawls of young people in a hurry, reflecting admiration and affection, reminiscing—looking toward the future, to college. . .and after.

Who could have anticipated?

Courtney Fielding's perfect young life was laid out before her on the pages of the burgundy leather-bound yearbook.

Rebecca closed it slowly and ran her fingers over the snarling tiger embossed on the smooth cover. She held it against her heart, tears gathering for the boy he once was and the dreams he had lost. *Dear God, heal his wounded spirit.*

"Why are you crying, Mommy?"

Davy was beside her, a worried expression on his face.

"I'm not crying, Davy."

"You are so."

"Not anymore." She dried her eyes with the back of her hand and returned the book to its place on the shelf.

As Davy and Ada continued to rummage expectantly through the bags and boxes, Rebecca drew away the sheets from a graceful set of bent-willow furniture that included a standing mirror, two chairs, a glass-topped coffee table and a chaise.

Ada glanced up. "That was the furniture in Miss Daisy's room when she was in high school."

"These too?" Rebecca asked, lifting the corner of one of the drapes that was folded in a pile on the chaise.

"Uh huh."

Scattered across the daffodil-yellow chintz was a garden of pale blue forget-me-nots and white lilies-of-the-valley. Even if she and Davy were only going to be there a short time more, she could just imagine the bent-willow furniture and the sunny curtains brightening the dour housekeeper's quarters below.

"You don't suppose Mr. Fielding would let me use them, do you?"

"Why not? This stuff's not doing anybody no good up here." Ada creaked upright, her hands in the small of her back. She stretched.

Rebecca smiled at Davy. "Don't you think this furniture looks a lot like what we have at home in the Philippines?"

"This is home," Davy said absently as he marched a tin soldier over a stack of books.

That hurt. If he only knew.

Ada glanced at Rebecca and quickly looked away.

How would Rebecca tell him they would be leaving? Long forgotten were Davy's words that first day when he'd asked why "that man" didn't want them. Since then he'd found Ada and Manuel, the caretaker, who allowed him to rake and plant radishes in the vegetable garden. And he'd uncovered the hidden heart of Courtney Fielding—the Courtney Fielding who drew pictures with him and read stories and zoomed through the mansion with Davy on his lap.

It would not be easy for Davy to leave paradise.

"Do you think Daisy would mind if I borrowed this furniture?"

"She wouldn't care at all. It was her grandmother's choice, not Miss Daisy's."

Rebecca fingered a corner of the drape and wondered, now that Courtney Fielding and Davy had formed such a close attachment, why he was still so eager to get rid of them.

Of course, after the morning's altercation it didn't take much imagination to figure it was not Davy, but Rebecca, who had come to be the reason.

And yet she got mixed messages from him. Often she had the feeling he was watching her. On several occasions when she and Davy were in the garden, she'd looked toward the library and seen him at the window. And other times, like last night at dinner, she'd glanced up and met his gaze. He'd abruptly turned away, as if he was embarrassed at being caught.

Other times he would look right at her and seem not to see her at all, his eyes reflective and, she thought, sad. There was something about that expression that touched her heart.

She sighed and began spreading out the drapes for closer scrutiny.

It was all probably just her imagination. Wishful thinking.

Wishful thinking?

Abruptly she turned her attention to examining the chintz. "Too bad," she said to Ada. "Silverfish have gotten into them, but it looks as if there's enough good fabric left for short curtains at the windows and to make a couple of slipcovers for the cushions of the chairs. Maybe two or three throw pillows. I could whip them up in a few hours on that Singer in the sewing room. I love this pattern. It's so cheerful. It would be a shame to waste it." She looked up. "Do you think he'd let me have it? Otherwise there won't be anything left except shreds."

"He wouldn't even know."

"I wouldn't think of not asking him." Rebecca frowned. "I hate to, though. I'm afraid of what he'll say, given our problems this morning."

"Yes is what he'll say, Miss Rebecca," Ada said, turning to Davy. "Start choosing what you're going to take, Davy. Your room won't hold it all. You can trade later if you get tired of something."

Rebecca began folding up the drapes. "I don't know, Ada. I don't think your Mr. Court is looking too kindly on me at the moment."

"He's probably already forgotten. Mr. Court don't hold a grudge." Ada began putting the blocks Davy had been playing with into their box. "Would you feel better if I asked him?"

"Would you?" Rebecca gave her an abashed smile. "I know I seem like a coward, but yes, I really would feel better. How about the furniture, too? Might as well go for it all."

"No harm in asking." With the support of a nearby chair Ada pushed herself to her feet. "Davy, you can come up with Manuel after your nap and tell him what you want him to carry down."

"I want the farm set now, Ada."

"No problem. Put 'em all back in the box, and I'll carry 'em for you. They'll be light enough."

"I'll carry this one," he said, clutching the billy goat he'd been holding.

Rebecca said, "I know you think it's silly to go to all the trouble when we're not going to be here that long, but whoever's in the room after us will enjoy it." She selected a few books for Davy from the boxes. "All right, you two—we've spent enough time for today."

Near the door she caught sight of a number of paintings stacked carelessly facing the wall. "Those look like gold-leaf frames, Ada. They shouldn't be treated that way, no matter what the paintings are like."

"They're Mr. Court's. He told me to throw 'em out, but I sneaked 'em up here."

"Maybe I can use them, too." Rebecca turned the top painting around. What she saw took her breath away. For a moment she couldn't speak. "Ada, this is beautiful."

"Mr. Court painted it."

"Did he paint the others, too?"

Ada nodded sadly.

Rebecca put down the stack of books and began turning the paintings, standing them side by side along the wall: plein air paintings in the jewel colors of the California landscape, fields of purple lupine and orange poppies; copses of sycamores, eucalyptus, and oaks; dew-sprinkled citrus groves glistening in the morning sun; the mauve San Gabriel Mountains against a clear cerulean sky. They were breathtaking in their beauty. Heartbreakingly lovely.

"Oh, Ada, how could he want to destroy them?"

fifteen

The yeasty smell of fresh baked bread drifted into the library, reminding Court it was almost time for lunch. He glanced up at the mantel clock above the fireplace and pushed his chair back from the desk. Rebecca made it a point to serve meals on time. A definite virtue. She was not only one terrific cook, but as an artist he appreciated the way she took such pains with the presentation. In contrast to Neda who threw decent but unimaginative food on the plate without a thought as to how it looked.

Rebecca could give her a few tips in that department.

Her cooking was not the only thing he would miss when she left. As he wheeled through the living room he paused, remembering what it was like before she arrived: the pulled drapes, the silence, the dimness, the musty smell a room gets when it hasn't been aired out or occupied. Now fresh flowers stood on the table behind the couch. The drapes rippled from the breeze wafting through the open windows. Treasures long forgotten or ignored were artfully arranged on the coffee table.

She'd made the dreary house a home again. And she had brought joy.

He gave the push rim a hard thrust and coasted across the oriental rug.

Now these rooms were filled with voices and laughter, the click of her heels, the patter of Davy's small feet.

She had brought life.

The wheels of his chair made a soft whoosh as they rolled across the tiled floor toward the dining room.

Yes, he would miss her welcoming smile as she poured his cup of coffee in the morning. He would miss seeing her strong slender figure striding past the library door. He would miss the weary, dreamy look in her large, brown eyes when she said good night.

It would be as if a match flickered and went out, when she finally left. He knew that.

But most of all he would miss their talks—even the heated ones. She showed fire and spunk. As she had last night when she'd stood up for Ada and again this morning when she'd stood up for herself. She was spontaneous and unexpected. Passionate. She made no accommodation for his disability. In fact, she seemed not to notice.

In the dining room he wheeled over to the arched window. Absently he locked his fingers in his lap as he gazed out over the cobbled drive and the sweeping stretch of lawn beyond.

With each day she had been there, he'd found his feelings for her deepening.

The truth was, he couldn't get enough of her. He would never get enough. He knew that. He was reconciled to it. That was the reason he couldn't let her stay. The sooner she left, the better off he would be in the long run. . .in the dull, empty long run.

❧

In the kitchen Rebecca paused to wipe her damp temple with the corner of her apron then resumed lifting the golden-brown crescents off the baking sheet and tucking them between the folds of a linen napkin in the silver breadbasket.

While Davy and Ada played a heated game of "I spy" at the kitchen table, she quickly tossed the dressing into the crab salad and piled it onto a lettuce-lined plate, garnishing it with wedges of avocado, tomato, and hard-cooked eggs. For good measure she added a sprig of parsley.

She hadn't seen her employer since breakfast and felt some trepidation. He was probably applauding his resolve to get rid of her. Who could blame him? A man might put up with such temerity from a wife, but certainly not from a servant. And that's what she was. She might as well get used to it. She was employed to do her work and keep her mouth shut—if she could manage.

If she didn't learn that lesson, her next employer wouldn't keep her long either.

She picked up the plate of crab salad in one hand and the basket of rolls in the other, gathered up her courage, and headed for the dining room.

Dear Lord, help me to hold my tongue, not snap to judgment, and mind my own business, she prayed then pushed open the door.

Courtney Fielding smiled at her. As she laid the plate down in front of him, his gaze locked with hers in tacit understanding that the morning's unpleasantness would be a thing of the past.

She felt greatly relieved. In the brief time she had left, she wanted him to think well of her. After all, as her employer, she might need him to give her a reference. That's what she told herself anyway. But that wasn't the only reason, and she knew it.

He snapped his napkin into his lap. "Up to your usual standard, I see."

"I hope that's a compliment."

"It is. Have you eaten yet?"

She nodded. For a moment she'd thought he was about to ask her to join him.

"Well, if it didn't poison you, I guess I can safely take a bite."

"Don't be too sure. I had a peanut butter sandwich for lunch."

Before she reached the door, he said, "Ada tells me Davy wasn't the only one to find things in the attic."

As he had that morning, it seemed again that he wanted her to stay.

She turned. "It was like Christmas. We even found a tricycle. But I think Davy's favorite was the tin farm. He wouldn't let go of the billy goat."

"My favorite, too, when I was his age. The tricycle was Daisy's." He frowned. "Sit down, Mrs. Spaneas. You make me nervous hovering by the door. You look like a filly ready to bolt."

Obediently Rebecca pulled out a chair at the farthest end of the table.

"Come closer. Being crippled is not contagious, you know." His voice was impatient, almost harsh.

Already the Lord was testing her. She had to bite her tongue not to snap back.

"Please," he added quietly, his gaze gentling, making amends.

Rebecca did as he bade but left a chair between them.

"She said you were taken with Daisy's old bedroom furniture." He took a sip of water, as if preparing his palate for the next bite. "And some curtains."

She nodded.

"Help yourself. You're welcome to anything up there that you want."

Anything? She was tempted to mention his paintings and thought better of it. "That's kind of you."

"What am I going to do with the stuff? Save it for my children?" His benign expression had a flash of bitterness. "Unlikely." He stabbed a wedge of egg.

"Why wouldn't you?"

"What?"

"Save it for your children?" she said.

He looked at her as if she had a few bolts missing in her brain. "First I need a wife, don't you think? And so far there isn't that much of a call for cripples."

It was as if he enjoyed assaulting himself with the word

cripple. As much as he attracted her, he aggravated her. He used his infirmity as an excuse and a shield. She'd experienced too much—seen too many die, including her own beloved husband. No, she wasn't buying it!

She didn't blink. "It's your choice, Mr. Fielding."

"Is it really? Do you really think—never mind. I'll have Manuel help you move things this afternoon," he said abruptly and speared a wedge of tomato.

Rebecca started to rise.

"Wait." He didn't look at her. "I'm sorry. Please stay," he said quietly.

Stiffly she lowered herself back into the chair, folding her hands tightly in her lap. Chiding herself. She was as much at fault as he for the awkwardness. Once again she had challenged him. And after her vow to mind her own business and keep her mouth shut—with God's help. She sighed. *Sorry, Lord, for the lapse.*

Courtney Fielding looked up. "Why are you going to so much trouble to decorate when—"

"—we're only going to be here such a short time?"

He nodded.

"As I told Ada, whoever moves in after us will enjoy it. There isn't that much to do really. The room just seems a bit"—*dank? depressing? dull? all of the above*—"in need of sprucing up. Besides, I love to decorate. I've been wanting an excuse to get my hands on that Singer sewing machine since I arrived."

"Uh huh. Quite the little domestic. That doesn't surprise me." He lifted another forkful of crab salad.

She studied him for a moment.

"What?"

She shrugged. "You just sounded—I don't know—a bit condescending, that's all," she said mildly. *Still, why did she have to say it at all?*

He looked surprised. "On the contrary. Being a home-maker is a big job. My mother left it to the servants and the decorators and the landscapers. I meant it as a compliment."

"In that case, I plead guilty. To the domestic part anyway. But I'm afraid I must take exception to the adjective *little*. I haven't been called little since I left the womb. You have to be pretty tall to call me that."

Oh, no. How insensitive am I? Will I never learn? She could feel the heat of chagrin. "I—uh—" *This is getting to be a disaster.*

He waited, his fork suspended, eyeing her as a collector eyes a mounted butterfly, still struggling on the pin.

"I did notice you have very long legs," she blurted out. "I mean. . ." She was digging the hole deeper. Now he would think she was mocking his handicap.

When she finally mustered the courage to look at him again, she found him smiling.

"Six feet two, to be exact. A hundred and eighty pounds."

He was teasing. What a relief. Who could figure from one minute to the next what he was thinking? If he only knew how attractive he was when he smiled.

He folded his napkin and patted his stomach. "As always, my compliments to the chef." He looked replete and satisfied.

"A piece of that chocolate cake for dessert?" She rose to clear his plate.

"Maybe later. When you've finished in the kitchen, come into the library. Paul and I stopped by the Department of Motor Vehicles on our way to the VA hospital. We picked up the pamphlet with the questions you'll need to know before you take the driver's test."

"That was thoughtful of you."

He wheeled toward the entry hall. "It's in my own best interests. And you'll be much more likely to get that job tomorrow if you have a driver's license."

Ah, Mr. Fielding, she thought, *why did you have to ruin it?*

sixteen

As soon as Court wheeled out of the elevator, he heard shuffling and footsteps from behind the door at the end of the hall. There was a thud, a dragging sound, and laughter. He would have given anything to be the one to help Rebecca move the furniture down from the attic. The fact that he could only sit helplessly confined in this wretched chair filled him once again with anger.

Nevertheless he was curious. Instead of going left into his bedroom, he turned right and pushed his wheelchair down the hall toward the servants' quarters.

Aside from a few isolated moments, he'd behaved pretty much like a jerk that day. It seemed the more intense his feelings, the more unpredictable and volatile his behavior. He didn't want Rebecca to leave remembering him that way. He was determined to turn over a new leaf, be more circumspect in his behavior.

He reached for the knob of the door that led to the hall between her rooms and the rest of the house. Before he could turn it, though, the door opened, and Rebecca stuck out her head.

"Oh, Mr. Fielding, it's you."

"You were expecting the tooth fairy?"

"I don't want you to come in until it's finished. I was hoping to surprise you. What time is it?"

He looked at his watch. "One-thirty."

"Come back at four. By then I should be done. Do you mind?"

Yes, he minded. But what could he say? If a new leaf was to be turned, it might as well be now.

"Very well." He tried not to sound irritated.

The door closed. But before he had a chance to turn his chair around it opened, and Rebecca's head popped out again.

"We'll have tea," she said.

Two and a half hours later Rebecca was all smiles as she invited Court into her newly decorated apartment.

It was amazing. What was once a dull, serviceable sitting room had been transformed into a garden of sunshine and flowers. Made even lovelier by the presence of its occupant.

Rebecca stood in front of him wearing a simple flower-print dress. He'd thought her beautiful before, but in this happy state she was lovelier than ever, her color high, her dark eyes sparkling with excitement.

"I knew there was enough fabric to make curtains and a valance," she said, "and slipcover the cushions of the two bent-willow chairs. But with a little clever patching I was able to eke out enough material to make these three throw pillows for the daybed. What do you think?"

"I think you're terrific!" He could see her fidget in his direct gaze and made the effort to pull his eyes away. "It's terrific."

Her voice was breathless as she continued. "Everything came from the attic except the drop-leaf table and those two chairs on either side and"—she pointed—"the daybed and that slipper chair in the corner. They were the only things here when we moved in."

"I'm afraid I wasn't paying that much attention," he said, struggling now to focus on her handiwork and not her. "I can only say, now it looks like a page out of *Good Housekeeping*."

"Hardly." Nevertheless Rebecca beamed. "But it's bright and sunny, and it makes me happy."

"If it makes you happy, I'm happy." That sounded a bit obsequious. He'd vowed to turn over a new leaf, not a whole tree. He shook his head and grinned. "And all these treasures were hidden in our attic. Which reminds me—where's your shadow?"

"Don't come in, Mr. Court," Davy called. "I don't want you to see my room. I'm not ready."

"Okay, Davy." Court smiled up at Rebecca. "Like mother, like son. Full of surprises."

She blushed in his lingering gaze. Abruptly she leaned down and reached for a small blue crackle-glass vase on the coffee table filled with a bouquet of weeds, sticks, and dandelions. "I found this in the attic. Davy contributed the arrangement. And this"—she put down the vase and touched a vintage pressed-glass plate—"charming little sculpture of a rabbit. Isn't it dear?"

Court laughed. "A precocious ten-year-old artist with the initials C. F. created that."

Rebecca's voice held a reflective softness. "I suspected as much." She smoothed the front of her dress. Without looking at him she said, "I believe I have other pieces by that artist."

It was then Court noticed the painting on the wall above the daybed.

He took a deep breath and expelled it slowly as he scanned the room. "I told Ada to get rid of them," he growled.

"What a sin that would have been," Rebecca said.

"I told her—"

"Oh, Mr. Fielding. God gave you such a gift. Why are you wasting it?"

He shrugged. "It's my gift. I suppose I can do with it as I please."

"I'm sorry, Mr. Fielding. I just don't agree with you at all."

"You rarely do."

Rebecca ignored him and went on. "God chose you for a reason. You have an obligation—"

"A gift with strings attached is hardly a gift."

"Have you forgotten the parable of the talents? Remember the twenty-fifth chapter of Matthew, verse twenty-nine? 'For unto every one that hath shall be given, and he shall have abundance: but from him that hath not shall be taken away even that which he hath.'"

"You read your books, Mrs. Spaneas. I'll read mine." He could feel the muscles in his jaw tightening. The woman had an opinion on everything. But this was an infringement.

Rebecca looked down at him, her eyes filled with sadness and compassion.

Her saving grace. Compassion. Inwardly he sighed.

"When I saw these paintings, Mr. Fielding, I began praying for you," she said quietly. "And I will continue, whether you like it or not, until you pick up a brush and start painting again."

"I'm flattered." He raised an eyebrow. "But don't you think you're being a bit presumptuous? How do you know God's intentions? Maybe He really wanted me dead with the rest of the men in my battalion, and the devil stepped in and saved me. Wanted me as a reminder that the Almighty isn't so almighty after all."

He could see he had shocked her, but she quickly gathered her composure.

"Now that *is* the devil speaking." She crossed her arms and looked down at him thoughtfully. "But you do have a point," she conceded. "Instead I'll pray that your closed heart is opened to receive God's plan for your life. How does that sound?"

"Better. But don't count on it. You aren't the first to offer prayers on my behalf. There's a long line before you. Most notably that pro, our own Pastor Jack. So far, sad to say, none of it has done much good."

"We'll see."

From the adjoining room Davy called, "I'm ready now."

Rebecca squinched up her pretty nose. "Do you mind? He's really been looking forward to showing you his treasures."

"Of course not." Court wheeled his chair around.

"While you do that, I'll bring up the tea. We can have it right here. Is that all right?"

"Perfect. Absolutely perfect." And he meant every word as he watched her walk out the door, her tall, graceful body, her slim waist and shapely legs.

She was all woman, for sure. He breathed a deep sigh. But more than that. She was all heart.

"Mr. Court, where are you?" Davy called impatiently.

Court wheeled into the small bedroom.

Davy was standing in the middle of the room wearing a cowboy hat and chaps a couple of sizes too large. A holster with a toy gun sagged from his belt. "You can call me Cowboy Davy," he said, in as deep a voice as small vocal chords could manage. "You be the bad guy, Mr. Court." He whispered in Court's ear, "We're just pretending," then reached for his gun.

"Don't shoot, Cowboy Davy!" Court yelled, shaking with fear as he lifted his hands above his head.

"Don't worry, Mr. Court," Davy said, momentarily stepping out of character. "Mommy says I can only scare bad guys. I don't really shoot 'em. Then I tie 'em up. But I don't have rope yet."

"Well, that's a relief." Court lowered his hands. "Ah, I see your sidekick George riding your horse in the corner."

"That's not a horse, Mr. Court. That's a tricycle." He glanced at Court as if he were mentally incapacitated. "Mommy says I can't ride it in the house."

"In that case, we'll have to find a place on the patio to park it," Court said.

Between the bookcase and a stack of blocks was the wicker toy box, partially open. Old Teddy's head stuck out from one corner.

"Mommy had to fix his eye," Davy said.

Court pointed to the tin box in the middle of the little table. "That looks familiar. Can I take a look at it?"

"It's a farm, Mr. Court." Davy picked up the box and returned, handing it to Court. "It has chickens and cows and pigs and a fence and a barn"—his voice lifted in delight as he explained—"and a farmer and—"

"I used to play with that farm when I was a boy your age, Davy," Court said.

"You can see inside if you're careful. Don't lose anything." Davy lifted the lid.

The two heads touched, as the man and boy riffled through the contents.

"I don't see Billy-Goat," Court said.

"Billy-Goat doesn't want to see anybody. Only me."

"Oh, I think he'd want to see me. We're old friends."

"I'll ask him." Davy reached into his pocket. He lifted his small fist and whispered into it. He held it to his ear.

"What did he say?" Court asked, very serious.

"He said not now."

Court frowned. "I'm very disappointed. Did you tell him who it was that wanted to see him?"

"I forgot." Davy went through the motions again, whispering, listening. "He said he'd see you when we have chocolate cake and tea."

"I guess I can wait until then."

They heard Rebecca's step on the back stairs.

"In the nick of time." Court pushed himself into the little sitting room as Rebecca set the tray on the table beneath the window.

"I want to eat at my own table, Mommy. Can I?" Davy asked.

"I don't see why not. We'll bring it in here with us."

Court watched as Rebecca helped Davy set his and George's places at the little table. She sliced two tiny pieces of cake which he insisted on carrying, inching across the floor with small, scuffling steps, the cake shifting precariously on the tilted plate.

With Rebecca hovering behind him, he carried first George's and then his cup of tea—only a hint—in a cup half full of warm milk. With her supervision he added a half-teaspoon of sugar to each.

"Ada calls it cambric tea," Davy informed Court as he stirred. "It's good for you, you know."

"That's what she used to tell me," Court said.

Rebecca leaned down and kissed the back of Davy's neck.

"*Mommy!*" Davy said with exasperation.

She winked at Court behind the boy's back. "Tastier than chocolate cake," she murmured.

Court understood. As she'd leaned forward, his gaze had followed the smooth curve of her neck. Chocolate cake wasn't even in the running.

She was infinitely patient but never condescending. Everything his own mother wasn't. His mother had had no time for patience, with all her harried social obligations. Court had always vowed he would marry a woman whose children came first. He was beginning to think he'd found her. But the Lord in all His wisdom had put her out of reach. Small wonder that he had such little regard for the Lord's wisdom.

Rebecca sat on the daybed, Court opposite, across the glass-topped coffee table. He had a second slice of cake, while she still nibbled her first. She filled his cup again, and hers, and his again, as they talked.

Davy went to play in his room with George.

Court found out about her life as a child growing up in affluence, the daughter of a plantation owner in the Philippines; she learned about his summers as a boy, here on the estate. They stopped short of discussing the war, the event that had decimated their lives, reshaped them, and brought them together. They talked until the crumbs had dried on their plates and the tea in their cups grew cold.

Wheeling out into the hall, Court said, "Tonight we'll eat in the solarium."

Rebecca was leaning against the open door. "Oh, is Jack coming to dinner again?"

"No. It will just be the three of us."

seventeen

The solarium was bathed in the fading pink of twilight. In the corner, overlooking the garden, Rebecca and Davy, who was still wearing his chaps with his holster hooked onto his belt, were setting the glass-top table—for three.

"—the three of us," Courtney Fielding had said.

She still could hardly believe she had heard him correctly. What a turnaround in the last twenty-four hours.

Davy counted, "One, two, three—where's Pastor Jack's place?"

"What makes you think Pastor Jack is coming?"

"We don't eat with Mr. Court if Pastor Jack don't—doesn't—come," Davy said, taking the salad forks from his mother and placing them carefully on the left side of the mats.

"Well, tonight we are. Are you disappointed?"

"It's okay." With meticulous care he began lining up the soupspoons on the opposite side. "I like Mr. Court. He's fun."

Rebecca looked down at him thoughtfully. "Well—I guess sometimes he is."

"I think he's fun all the time. He says I can park my tricycle on the patio. What are we having for dinner?"

"We had such a late tea, just something simple. Tomato soup, cheese bread and Waldorf salad."

"Wal—wal—is that the one with nuts? George doesn't like nuts."

"I'll make his without them. Now go to the library, knock politely on the door, and tell Mr. Court that I'm ready to serve dinner."

As Rebecca was spooning the salad into lettuce leaves, Davy dashed back into the kitchen. "Mr. Court said wait

121

five minutes. Me and him are going in the elevator to get my tricycle."

Since that first day she had avoided the elevator with Davy. She could foresee all sorts of problems if he decided it was fun, the way riding a carousel is fun or the little bouncy car at the market. But he was out of the kitchen before she could impart the threats and warnings that were a mother's obligation. She just hoped Courtney Fielding hadn't started something they'd all be sorry for later.

As she heated the soup and stuck the cheese bread under the broiler to melt, she reflected on the roller coaster of a day she'd had. Earlier, when she sat across from Courtney Fielding in the cheerful setting of her newly decorated room, she'd quite forgotten he was her employer. She'd felt she was conversing with an old friend. It was that comfortable. She'd had more than a glimpse of the boy he once was: the one on the donkey, the one in the yearbook, the cheeky young lieutenant. She understood now why Ada adored him.

He had charm. He also had intelligence and wit and a unique gentleness. She had glimpsed it before in the way he treated Davy. That afternoon she saw it in the way he treated her.

She pulled the bread from the broiler and lowered the flame under the soup to a simmer. She could hear his and Davy's voices in the hall as they got out of the elevator.

She entered the solarium just in time to catch Davy peddling across the tiles on his tricycle. "Young man, what did I say about riding your tricycle in the house?"

"Mr. Court said I could."

Rebecca threw Courtney Fielding an exasperated look.

He smiled and shrugged.

"Besides," Davy said, "Mr. Court gets to ride all the time, so why can't I?"

She was about to say, because Mr. Court has to, but said instead, "It's Mr. Court's house. He can do anything he likes." She looked at Davy severely. "I suspect you forgot to tell him your mother's rule."

Averting his eyes, Davy hunkered down on his tricycle and thrust out his lower lip.

"I thought so."

Courtney Fielding zipped by, came to an abrupt stop, and pulled open the sliding glass door. "Better put that trike out to pasture, Cowboy Davy, before the damsel gets even more distressed."

Davy pumped past him and parked just outside the window where he could keep an eye on his new machine.

Rebecca laughed. "I wonder why I feel as if there are forces conspiring against me?" She eyed the sock monkey in Courtney Fielding's lap. "Ah, I see you've finally made friends with George. That's a good sign."

"Well, I thought it was safer than his riding sidesaddle on Cowboy Davy's trike."

Davy swung his leg over the tricycle seat and swaggered back into the house.

Rebecca suppressed a smile. "If you two hombres will sashay over to the chuck wagon, I'll rustle you up some grub."

When Rebecca had finished saying the blessing, Court asked Davy, "Where did you learn all this cowboy stuff?"

"Grandpa Will gave me a book about 'em."

Rebecca laughed. "Dad said since we were heading west we might run into cowboys and Indians and we'd better be prepared."

"I'll have to take you to a Gene Autry movie." Court helped himself to the cheese bread.

By the time they had finished dinner, stars were just starting to sparkle in the periwinkle sky. It was bright enough with the light borrowed from inside the solarium for Davy to take a turn around the patio on his tricycle, with Courtney Fielding's supervision, while Rebecca cleaned up after dinner.

When she returned a few minutes later, she could hardly believe what she saw. With whoops and hollers, Courtney Fielding and Davy were racing recklessly back and forth across the lighted expanse.

Men! Rebecca could foresee disaster.

If she hadn't called out, it might not have happened. But she did. They both turned, and Courtney Fielding's wheelchair sailed over the edge of the patio, bounced down the three steps, and landed in the grass, his chair on top of him, its wheels spinning.

Davy pulled up short and watched in mute surprise as Rebecca ran across the patio and down the steps.

"Oh, Mr. Fielding, are you all right?"

She heard a mumbled response, and the wheelchair tipped upright.

"Just lie still. Let me help you," she cried.

"I'm fine," he muttered. "I'm all right." He rolled over, spitting grass. "Fool thing for me to do."

"Please, let me help—" She reached down.

"I'm perfectly capable of taking care of myself!" He pushed away her hand.

Rebecca staggered backward. Her heel caught on the edge of a sprinkler, and over she went. The next thing she was aware of was Courtney Fielding's anguished voice.

"Rebecca."

He was close enough for her to smell the minty scent of his breath, the warmth of his body hovering over hers, his hand against her cheek.

"Mrs. Spaneas, Rebecca—oh, my dear girl—are you all right? Say something."

It occurred to her to keep her eyes closed. Lie there, feeling the touch of his hand, listening to the sound of his voice, the sensation of his warm breath against her cheek. It was lovely, like some out-of-body experience that she wanted to last.

Then she heard Davy's frightened cry, "Mommy!" And she felt his little hand on her arm. She opened her eyes. "I'm okay, Davy. Don't worry."

"Oh, Rebecca."

Had she heard correctly? Had Courtney Fielding just called her Rebecca?

He laid a restraining hand on her shoulder. "Give yourself a minute. Don't get up too quickly, until you know you're all right."

She took a moment to be assured that she was, then pushed herself up on her elbows. "Ouch." She rubbed her hip. "That'll be black and blue. Are you all right, Mr. Fielding?"

"I'm okay. But I'm *really* sorry. I didn't think I pushed you that hard."

"You didn't. I tripped."

Courtney Fielding flopped back onto the grass. "If I hadn't acted like such a kid in the first place, it never would have happened. I'm really sorry."

She looked down at his hand, lying in the grass next to hers. If she moved her little finger. . .just an inch. . .they'd be touching.

Her gaze tracked up his arm, across his shoulder, and up the fulcrum of his neck. His features stood out in stark contrast, shadow and light, as she followed the line of his jaw, the cleft in his chin, his nose. . .and found his blazing blue eyes.

Rebecca's breath caught.

She felt their fingers touch. Had he moved, or she?

Davy jumped into her lap. "When you fell down, you scared me, Mommy."

"Didn't mean to, Honey." She wrapped her arms around him.

"That was some trick, Mr. Court," he said, over Rebecca's shoulder. "Maybe next time you can do it without tipping over."

"One trick too many, I'm afraid, Davy." He gave Rebecca a guilty smile. "If I try it again, your mom won't let me come out and play with you anymore."

"Why not? It was great."

"I suspect she thinks a responsible adult should show better judgment."

"What does that mean?"

"It means I need to behave myself."

"You behave yourself. Doesn't he, Mommy?"

Rebecca smiled. "Sometimes." She looked down at the man beside her and shook her head. "What a wild child you must have been."

He rose up on his elbow, resting his chin on his coiled fist. "I guess I did keep the servants jumping. Especially Ada. But she was tough. She could take it. Of course she was a lot younger then." He stopped suddenly and looked at her, silent for a minute. Then he said, "Would you be offended if I called you 'Rebecca'?"

She shrugged. "Of course not. You call Ada, Ada."

"It's not quite the same," he said quietly.

"Whatever you feel comfortable with, Mr. Fielding."

"In that case, one thing I'm sure of, I don't feel comfortable having you call me Mr. Fielding."

"How about you call him Mr. Court, Mommy, like Ada and me do?"

"That sounds reasonable," Rebecca said. "I could live with that."

"I'm not sure I could." Courtney Fielding lay back in the grass and lifted his eyes to the stars then turned again toward Rebecca. "But it's a step in the right direction."

She smiled down at him. "What direction is that, Mr. Court?"

"Leave off the 'Mister.' Just call me Court."

"Is that a request or a demand?"

"Whatever works." His eyes, smoldering blue fire in the dimness, burned into hers. "It never has seemed right, this formality. Our sisters are best friends after all." Suddenly he grinned. "As I recall, when Imogene was a sophomore in college, I even spent one delightful evening with her at our family's annual Christmas party."

"So I heard." Rebecca returned his grin. "Why do you think I came here?"

He turned serious. "If we'd met under any other circumstance, it would have been Court and Rebecca. Look, Rebecca—we got off to a bad start for lots of reasons. None of them yours. You've been fine. More than fine, in spite of it. You and Davy aren't going to be here much longer. I don't want it to end the way it began."

If someone had asked Rebecca at that moment, sitting there in a moonlit night under the stars, bathed in the heady perfume of honeysuckle, beside this complicated, interesting—beautiful—man, she would have had to admit that, regardless of how it began, she wasn't at all anxious for it to end.

❧

Rebecca sat on the edge of Davy's bed waiting for him to finish brushing his teeth and reflecting on the evening just past. There was no denying that she was strongly attracted to Courtney Fielding, and from every indication the feeling was mutual.

"I'm finished, Mommy." Davy ran in from the bathroom, grabbed George, and knelt by the side of his bed.

Rebecca dropped down next to him. Together they bowed their heads. Hearing his sweet voice recite his prayers each night never ceased to choke her with emotion.

"Now I lay me down to sleep; I pray the Lord my soul to keep. If I should die before I wake, I pray the Lord my soul to take. God bless Mommy, and Daddy in heaven, and Gramma and—" The list went on.

"You forgot Ada," she reminded him.

"I didn't forget—and Ada and Pastor Jack. And especially, God, bless Mr. Court and make his legs work so we can do more things together like run races and go fishing. Amen."

Yes, please, Lord. Silently Rebecca echoed his prayer.

Davy jumped into bed, tucking George next to him and putting his thumb in his mouth, and closed his eyes.

Rebecca kissed both lids, the tip of his nose, his sweet, pointy chin. She loved that squeaky clean smell fresh out of his bath. She smoothed the covers around him. As always, she watched until his eyes closed and she heard the steady, gentle breathing of sleep.

Gazing down on his dark curls, she was reminded, as always, of David, his father. Her beloved husband.

Her attraction to Courtney Fielding surely was a betrayal of that memory. A cord of guilt tightened around her heart as she realized that recently she had thought of David more in terms of the past, than the present or the future.

Could she attribute that to her attraction to Court? The two men were nothing alike. Her husband, David, had been calm, controlled, dependable, his behavior exemplary. Always. Court Fielding was volatile and unpredictable. From one day to the next, she didn't know what to expect.

She smiled wryly. The difference in temperament between an engineer and an artist.

Nevertheless she could hardly hold a man like Court up as a paragon of virtue for Davy to emulate. Not as she had David. She had yet to find a man alive who could meet her dead husband's virtues.

That was an irony she hesitated to admit.

The only one who came close was Jack. And even he seemed more earthbound than David had been.

Rebecca strongly believed that God had a purpose for everyone's life. She pondered what purpose there was in having her come to this place. And then it occurred to her. Perhaps it was not she but Davy who had been sent by God. Sent as a conduit for His unconditional love, to unlock the door to Courtney Fielding's wounded heart.

eighteen

Court had overslept. Or so he told Rebecca when she knocked on the bedroom door the next morning to bring him a mug of coffee and to ask him if he wanted her to hold breakfast.

Since he was late, he'd just make do with the coffee, thanks.

In the raw light of day the impetuous yearnings of a moonlit night showed tarnish. That casual intimacy that had seemed so natural at the time now struck him as a big mistake. It bred too many expectations, too much hope.

A sharp knock interrupted his reflections. "It's me, Mr. Court, Paul. We're gonna be late again."

"I'll be down in a minute."

The reality was that Rebecca's and Davy's presence was a momentary diversion. To hope for more was only courting heartbreak. When they left, nothing would have changed. He would still be a cripple with little to give and less to look forward to.

As usual he fought with himself as to whether even to bother with therapy that day. And, as usual, he found himself pushing his wheelchair toward the elevator. Why, he thought, did that still small voice within him refuse to let him give up?

Downstairs he took a detour by way of the solarium. Rebecca and Davy were finishing breakfast. There was another place setting at the table—by his direction—untouched.

Davy's face lit up. "Hi, Mr. Court—we missed you."

Rebecca glanced up but didn't smile. "Good morning."

"Sorry about breakfast." He tossed her a set of car keys. "Thought you might prefer to take the Cadillac for your driving test, since it's the car you'll be using while you're here."

"Thank you."

"Ada expects to take care of Davy," he said.

Rebecca started to rise. "I told you yesterday—"

"She and I have already discussed it." He forced a smile. "You wouldn't want to disappoint her." He started toward the door. "Oh, and good luck with your interview. I hope you get the job." With that he turned and wheeled out of the room.

&

Rebecca stared after him.

Had last night been a dream?

No! She wasn't that crazy.

Regardless of the reason, he was back to his old ways. Not rude. Not mean. Perfunctory, without any of the warmth and charm he'd displayed the night before. A mix of anger and embarrassment curdled in her stomach. How could she have been so—so seduced by an illusion? He'd blindsided her again.

Still, her heart told her he wasn't all sham. She'd seen too much evidence otherwise. It made her sad. He still had a lot of healing ahead of him, and it had nothing to do with his legs.

An hour later she was ready and waiting when the doorbell rang. Jack stood in the entry, his open, good-natured face a welcome sight. Even in his dark clerical suit he looked less somber than Court Fielding had in a bright Hawaiian shirt that—it occurred to her at the time—must have been a gift. It was too cheerful a choice for him to have made for himself.

"I am so glad to see you," Rebecca said, drawing Jack into the entry hall. The clasp of his big hands felt substantial and comforting. At least here was a man whose moods she could count on.

"I wanted to get here early so you could practice your parallel parking." He grinned.

"Let me just grab my purse and say good-bye to Davy." She returned a couple of minutes later dangling the car keys. "Court said we should drive the Cadillac."

"Doesn't think my old Dodge will engender enough confidence in the examiner, huh." Jack smiled. "Can't say as I blame him." He pulled open the front door. "So it's Court now. It's about time. And I hope you're Rebecca instead of Mrs. Spaneas."

She shrugged. "For the time being. Who knows? The man is so unpredictable." As they walked down the front steps, she said, "Sometimes I feel guilty; I get so impatient with him. He's so moody. Last night he was one person, this morning another. Clearly he believes people define him by his handicap." She sighed. "Not those whose opinions are worth anything. If he only knew. It's so sad."

They paused at the bottom of the steps.

Jack gave her a probing look. "It sounds as if you've come to care about him quite a bit—in spite of himself."

"He makes it hard, that's for sure."

"You're not answering my question."

"It was a question? Davy adores him." The way Jack was looking at her, Rebecca knew that answer didn't satisfy him either. "I do appreciate how good he is with Davy." She looked down at the clutch bag in her hand. "How much can you care about someone who won't let you know him? I pray for him."

"So do I." Jack gazed at her a moment longer then turned and walked toward the garage.

He lifted the heavy garage door with one hand. Inside, on the left, was a vintage Lincoln limousine.

"Old Mrs. Fielding used to cruise around Pasadena with her chauffeur in livery," Jack said.

Next to the Lincoln was a red Cadillac convertible.

"Court's grandmother gave it to him when he enlisted. She figured with that car as an incentive he'd make it home."

"Did she live to know how close he came to not making it?" Rebecca asked.

"No, she died the next summer." He opened the door on the driver's side. "Milady."

A few swings down and back on the long driveway and some parking practice was all Rebecca needed to feel comfortable and in control of the smoothly operating vehicle. On their way to the DMV, she reviewed the pamphlet Court had given her for the written exam.

It was nearly eleven o'clock by the time she had completed both tests and her temporary driver's license was tucked safely into her wallet.

Jack took over the wheel. "The convalescent hospital isn't far out of our way to the restaurant. I thought we'd stop by there first, and you can meet Miss Bufford."

As they entered the front door, they were slapped with the heavy, acrid stench characteristic of convalescent hospitals. At the desk the receptionist, her face frozen in a frown that reflected her irritation at being interrupted, directed them to "Room five, down the hall to the right."

Miss Bufford was a delicate wisp of a lady with gray curls, once blonde, and a pretty face, delicate and lined as handmade lace.

"We're friends of Dr. Emerson," Jack said.

"Oh, yes." She blessed them with a bright smile. "Reverend George told me you might be coming."

Jack took the elderly lady's extended hand in his two great paws and introduced Rebecca and himself.

Beneath the covers, the bulge of her cast seemed to take up

as much space on the bed as the diminutive Miss Bufford.

"It makes jumpin' rope a bit difficult." Her crackly voice reminded Rebecca of Ada, but with a genteel Southern softness.

Rebecca was drawn to her at once.

"Your lunch, Honey." A young aide scurried past them carrying a tray that she placed on the bed table. She swung it around in front of Miss Bufford.

"Thank you, Margaret," the elderly lady said cheerily.

"We'll come back when you've eaten lunch," Rebecca said.

"No, no. Sit down." Miss Bufford lifted the cover on the plate. "Brown green beans and dry Salisbury steak." She made a face and replaced the lid. "It won't get worse with time, believe me. I'd invite y'all to join me, but you wouldn't want to." She turned to Rebecca. "Tell me about yourself. The reverend said you have a little boy. How old is he?"

"Davy's four," Rebecca said. Briefly she filled Miss Bufford in on her background in the Philippines, how she happened to come stateside and about Davy.

"Well, the child's no problem for me," Miss Bufford said. "I love little ones. Taught kindergarten for forty years. Did Reverend George tell you there's a guest cottage on the property?"

Jack nodded.

"Only one bedroom, but quite a nice size living room. A bathroom, of course, and a kitchenette. You could make your own meals, if you like—that's assuming you and I can reach an agreement."

Rebecca smiled. "So far it sounds promising." Her heart was beginning to beat faster at the possibility.

"I have no family left," Miss Bufford said. "My uncle had no children either. I inherited his estate. It's modest, but I manage to live comfortably. I like my privacy. If it hadn't been for this"—she knocked on her cast—"I'd be able to get along quite nicely alone, thank you. But at my age, my doctor doesn't trust me by myself. He's like a mother hen." She looked Rebecca over. "You just may be the answer to his prayers."

"To both our prayers," Rebecca said softly. "Not everyone welcomes a four year old."

"You know, of course, that you wouldn't be starting for at least two months," Miss Bufford said.

"That isn't a problem." She wouldn't have thought so last night. Since this morning she wasn't so sure.

Miss Bufford's glance scanned the sparse antiseptic hospital room. "When I leave, I won't be missing this garden spot. That's for certain."

Jack stood. "It's time you ate your lunch, Miss Bufford. May Rebecca and I visit you again?"

"I'd welcome it," she responded. "Maybe we can find a way to sneak in that boy of yours so I can get a look at him," she said to Rebecca. "Well, I've nattered on long enough." She turned her shrewd blue eyes on Jack. "I can see this young man is anxious to get you to himself."

Rebecca laughed. "He's my minister."

"No weddin' band on his finger. I may not be able to walk, but there's nothing wrong with my eyesight."

Rebecca glanced at Jack. His face had turned crimson.

It appeared Miss Bufford had hit close to the mark.

❧

Stepping from the stultifying odors of the convalescent hospital, they both paused on the front step and drew a deep, satisfying lungful of fresh air, looked at each other, and laughed.

"Fresh air! One of the most underrated of God's blessings," Jack said. "You don't appreciate it until you're deprived of it."

"Like most things, I guess," Rebecca said.

"It looks as if you'll likely get the job. Congratulations."

"Thanks." It seemed perfect. Just as it had been described.

"Do you want to drive, or shall I?" Jack asked as they walked across the parking lot.

"You drive," she said.

When they reached the car, he opened the door for her then went around, slid into the driver's seat, and stuck the key into the ignition. "Well, how do you feel about it?"

"The job? Oh, fine."

"You don't seem as enthusiastic as I thought you'd be."

She gave him an abashed look. "I should be, I know. It sounds just right for us. And I certainly like Miss Bufford. We'll get used to it."

"Is that the best you can say? You'll get used to it?" He put the car in reverse and backed out of the parking space.

Rebecca gazed out the window. "It's just that I can't understand why Mr. Field—why Court is still so anxious to have us leave."

Jack paused, his hand resting on the gearshift. "I'm not sure he fully understands that himself."

Rebecca turned and faced the pastor. "I've really tried to please him—"

"And you have."

"—and Davy's so happy there. And he's been such a good boy. I know Court was worried in the beginning about having a small child there, but Davy doesn't seem to bother him anymore. In fact, he truly seems to enjoy him. And Davy adores Court—loves him."

"What about you, Rebecca?"

"What about me?"

"All this talk about how Davy feels—how do you feel?"

"Does it matter?"

"It matters to me," Jack said quietly.

As Rebecca gazed into the man's kind brown eyes, she saw, as she had suspected, that Miss Bufford's instincts had been right. He wanted to be more than her pastor or her friend. He was looking at her as a man looks at a woman he cares about in a very particular way.

"I don't know how I feel. I honestly don't."

He held her gaze for a long moment then shifted into gear. "Well, you'll have two months to find out."

They drove to an intimate little restaurant with fresh flowers on linen-clad tables that were tucked among sweet-smelling citrus for alfresco dining.

"You couldn't have picked a more perfect spot," she said.

"I hope the food will measure up to the ambiance."

She smiled. "I have no doubt."

When the waiter arrived, she deferred to Jack to make their choices.

He took his time scanning the menu. "How does zucchini coriander soup sound to start? Served with goat cheese toasts."

"Delicious," she said.

"The carpaccio comes highly recommended."

"I don't know that I've ever had that."

The waiter leaned forward. "We use only the highest quality beef fillet," he explained. "It's cut into very thin strips and pounded even thinner, then layered in a bed of arugula. The dressing is simple but superb. A blend of marinated artichoke hearts, fresh lemon juice and olive oil drizzled over the carpaccio, which is, finally, garnished with Parmesan curls. I don't think you'll be disappointed."

"It sounds wonderful. I'll have mine rare, please," Rebecca said.

The waiter smiled indulgently and glanced at Jack.

"Indeed you will," the minister said. "Carpaccio is raw beef fillet."

"Oh."

"Do you want something else?"

"That's what you're having?"

He nodded.

"Oh, why not? I know if I don't order it, I'll be sorry."

"Good for you." Jack closed his menu and handed it to the waiter. "We'll have espresso granita for dessert. And bring us a couple of iced teas, please."

Rebecca looked around at the elegantly attired customers then down at her flower-print dress. The best she had, simple by any standards, and especially in comparison to the other patrons.

Before the war she wouldn't have thought twice about lunching in such sumptuous surroundings. How times had changed.

It suddenly occurred to her that it also seemed mighty fancy for a minister whose salary depended on what the collection plate held.

She frowned. "Jack, this place—"

"—seems rich on a minister's pay? Oh, it is. But you're worth it. Every exorbitant penny."

"Oh, Jack. I feel terrible. If you think I'm the kind of woman who—"

"Of course I don't." He reached his hand across the table and covered hers. He grinned. "But Court does. We're his guests. He said you've earned it."

Rather than being pleased, Rebecca was irritated. "This is exactly what I meant about the man's moods. One minute he's so cold that icicles wouldn't melt on his nose; the next minute he does something like this."

"As I said, I wish you could have known him before." Absently the minister played with his fork. "He didn't use to be that way. War does terrible things to people."

Rebecca lifted her eyes. "At least he's alive," she replied quietly.

nineteen

Rebecca and Jack didn't get back to the house until after three.

"Aren't you coming in?" she asked. "I know Court will want to see you."

"I'd like to, but I have to make an appearance at the Women's Guild. After that, the high school kids are having a sports night and potluck."

She smiled. "You will have had a busy day. I can't tell you how grateful I am for all you've done for me. For all of us. Court especially. He'll be greatly relieved to have us out of his hair."

"I wouldn't be too sure about that. I suspect when he hears you probably have the job, reality will set in. By his own admission, Rebecca Spaneas will be hard to replace."

"That's kind of you to say."

"I'm not being kind. I'm being honest." Jack's lingering gaze told her he meant it, in more ways than he was prepared to say. "Thank Court for lunch. Tell him I'll call him tomorrow."

"I will." She stood in the doorway watching him lope down the steps and across the drive. He waved as he climbed into his car.

Rebecca went into the house and closed the front door behind her. She leaned back against it, collecting her courage to face the lion in his lair. The entry hall was cool, alive with rainbows dancing off the crystal chandelier. It was filled with the scent of the roses she'd arranged before breakfast in the cut-glass vase on the center table.

As she listened to Davy's and Ada's quiet voices in the solarium, she thought back to the day she and Davy arrived. Over a month ago now. At just about this time. How muted and musty the mansion had seemed, steeped in melancholy.

"Dear God," she prayed softly, "don't let it be that way when we're gone. Let Your light continue to flood these rooms with love until it seeps into Court Fielding's heart. Help him find peace and purpose in his life."

Davy poked his head around the solarium door. "I thought it was you, Mommy. Come see what me and Ada colored."

The older lady appeared behind him. She leaned over and took his arm. "Hush, Davy. Remember what I told you. You have to be real quiet. Mr. Court is having one of his spells."

"I'm so sorry," Rebecca said softly.

"Is that you, Rebecca?" The lion's muffled voice sounded more like a mew than a roar.

Rebecca looked sternly at Davy and lifted her finger to her lips. "Shh." She put her face close to the library door. "Davy's sorry he bothered you."

"Come in."

She handed her hat and purse to Ada and entered the darkened room. The drapes were drawn. It took a moment for her to adjust to the dimness.

Court was reclining on the couch, his forearm flung across his eyes. "Davy's been okay. That's the first time I've heard him today. How did everything go?"

"Good. But we can talk about it later. I'm so sorry you're not feeling well. Can I get you anything? A cold compress? Some tea?"

"Maybe later. I'm better than I was. Took some medicine the doctor prescribed. Sit down."

Rebecca balanced on the edge of the ottoman.

"Did you pass your driver's test?" He kept his arm across his eyes as he spoke.

"Uh huh. It wasn't as difficult as I'd expected."

He was silent for a moment; then he asked, "How did your interview go?"

Ah, the real reason he'd called her in here. Even with his migraine, he couldn't wait to find out.

"The interview went very well. Miss Bufford is the lady's name. She seems very nice. She taught kindergarten for forty years. Loves children—"

He broke in. "So I gather you got the job." His voice had an edge.

"It looks that way. . .if I want it."

"Why wouldn't you? It sounds ideal."

Rebecca didn't answer at once. "It won't start for about two months. That's when Miss Bufford gets out of the convalescent hospital. Unfortunately I'm afraid you're stuck with us until then. If that's okay."

"Of course it's okay." He looked up at her from beneath his lifted arm. "It's not a matter of being stuck with you, as you put it."

What is it then, she wanted to ask, but gazed back at him in silence.

He covered his eyes again.

The minutes ticked by to the rhythm of the clock on the mantle.

Finally Court asked, "How did you like the restaurant?"

"Lovely."

"You don't sound very impressed."

"I was. It was lovely."

"I'm glad you enjoyed it. It's one of my favorites."

"Then you should have joined us."

He didn't respond. After a minute he said, "Did Jack try the carpaccio as I suggested?"

"We both did."

"Did you like it?"

"I've never had it before. I ordered it rare."

He attempted a smile and winced. "Lucky you didn't order it well-done."

Rebecca knelt beside him. "Would you like me to massage the back of your neck? That used to help my husband. He suffered from migraines, too." She reached up and with practiced fingers began to gently rub the base of Court's neck.

He moaned with relief.

"I think you'd be more comfortable if you didn't lie quite so flat," she said, after a number of minutes.

He boosted himself higher, arranging the pillows behind his back, as Rebecca leaned over him, adjusting those beneath his head.

"Is that better?"

He nodded, his eyes closed.

She sat down next to him on the edge of the couch. With deep, gentle strokes of her thumb and fingers, she kneaded the muscles along his shoulders. "No wonder you're hurting. Your muscles are so tight they twang." She continued massaging until she felt them begin to loosen. Then with the sides of her hands close together, she delivered light, quick karate-chops, first along the crest of the left shoulder, then the right, then massaged them again. "Can you feel the difference?"

"Uh huh."

Her hands moved up his neck, kneading gently, working the cords until they too relaxed, until his head sank deeper into the pillow and moved easily from side to side in her cupped hands.

"You're a miracle worker," he murmured thickly.

"Shh. I'm not finished."

"It'd suit me if you never finished."

She could have responded to that, but she didn't. She leaned over him, rotating her thumbs gently against his temples. Then, spreading her fingers through his thick dark hair, she massaged his scalp.

Every muscle seemed to melt as he sank deeper into the soft cushions of the couch.

Finally, with feathery strokes, she gently ran her fingertips over his face, her gaze following where they touched.

The thick dark lashes of his closed eyes curled along the summit of his cheekbones. She watched him take a deep breath, his chest expanding as he drew in the lungful of air, his lips parting slightly as it escaped on a protracted sigh.

She was studying his face so intently, so intimately, that it took a moment for her to register that he had opened his eyes and now stared back at her with an intensity that made her shiver.

Where his breathing had assumed a profound and steady pace, Rebecca's breath suspended.

His expression warmed as he continued to scan her face with the same minute attention she had studied his.

He reached up and tucked a loose strand of hair behind her ear.

He had relaxed at her gently probing touch. But when Court's hand carelessly grazed her cheek, every nerve in Rebecca's body tensed, every muscle tightened.

He caught and held her gaze. Lightly, almost indifferently, he said, "If I had known the extent of your talents, I might have discouraged you from leaving."

If he had known her talents? He'd certainly been given plenty of opportunity. For whatever reason, he hadn't bothered to notice, or didn't want to.

Abruptly she rose. "You look better. I'm glad I could be of help."

"Don't go yet." He sat up.

She glanced at the clock. "It's almost four-thirty. Ada's going to be leaving. I have to start getting dinner ready. You know how testy you get when you're not fed on time." She gave him a brief, noncommittal smile and tried for an expression that would brook no argument.

He shrugged. "We'll eat in the solarium then."

"The three of us?"

He nodded. "Of course."

She couldn't resist. "After you missed breakfast, Davy will be very disappointed if you don't make it to dinner."

"I'll make it."

She stepped around his wheelchair that was positioned within reaching distance at the end of the couch. As she passed his desk, she paused. She took a step back and a couple of deep breaths. Tilting her head, she said, "Court, do you smell something funny?"

He straightened and looked over the back of the couch. He sniffed. "No."

She moved closer to the desk. "There is definitely a strange odor."

Court pulled the wheelchair closer and hoisted himself up into it. He wheeled around the edge of the couch and over beside Rebecca.

"It has kind of a fishy smell. Can you smell it now?" she asked.

"Oh, no." He moaned. He pulled open the bottom left-hand drawer and pointed inside. "My lunch."

Rebecca peered over his shoulder at what looked like something wrapped in a linen napkin. "What is it?"

"One of Ada's famous tuna sandwiches."

"What's it doing there? You love Ada's tuna sandwiches."

"That's what she thinks. After all these years it would break her heart to know I can't stand them."

"So you hide them in your desk drawer?" Rebecca made a face.

Court nodded. "Yeah. Then I flush 'em down the toilet.

Obviously today I forgot."

"How long have you been pulling this subterfuge?"

"Let's see." He frowned. "I'd say since I was about eight."

Rebecca laughed and shook her head. "Sneaky guy."

"That wild child you were talking about." He gave her a weak smile.

"No wonder you had a migraine. You didn't get your lunch. You don't need a housekeeper; you need a mother." Or a wife.

Their smiles dimmed as she met his gaze. Once again there passed between them that spark of understanding that went beyond words.

Could she survive two more months of this?

Lightly she said, "May I do the honors this time?"

"As long as Ada doesn't find out, be my guest." He rolled his chair back.

"I can be as wily as you."

"I doubt that."

As she lifted the sandwich from the bottom drawer, what was beneath caught her eye. "Are those drawings?"

Before Court could react, she had put down the linen-wrapped sandwich and reached into the drawer again. From it she drew a stack of drawings.

He moved forward. "I'd rather you didn't—"

But it was too late; she had already spread them out on the desk: pencil sketches of a contemporary child that looked very much like Davy, in ancient biblical settings.

"So this is what you do when you eavesdrop on us in the evening." She turned to him. "Court, these are beautiful."

She came to the bottom of the pile. Three pictures left.

One by one she laid them on the desk.

Her breath caught.

They were exquisite, tender drawings that went beyond the medium of pencil and paper and spoke to the heart.

They were pictures of Rebecca and Davy.

"Oh, Court," she breathed, laying her hand on his shoulder. "They're beautiful."

She wondered if they were a result only of his talent, or if they also reflected deeper feelings for her and Davy? Perhaps those small signs—the lingering look, the brush of a hand—had not been her imagination after all.

Only time would tell.

But time was running out.

twenty

Not many nights after she'd discovered the tuna sandwich and the drawings, as was her habit, Rebecca knocked on the library door before going up to bed. Court didn't answer. The door was slightly ajar, and she could see the desk lamp still burning and part of the back of the wheelchair parked next to the couch. She knocked again. Worried when he still didn't respond, she pushed open the door.

She found him asleep on the couch. The afghan that had covered him lay in a heap on the floor. She hesitated to wake him, picked up the afghan and tucked it loosely around him.

Even in sleep his face was troubled. A muscle in his jaw jerked convulsively. He groaned and flung his head to one side in the throes of a bad dream.

"Court," she said softly, touching his arm. "Court—"

Suddenly he sat bolt upright.

Startled, Rebecca stepped back.

"Get down!" he shouted. "It's an ambush. Move back, men!" His eyes were open, but blind to his surroundings.

He leaned forward, listening, turning, tracking the sounds that only he could hear. "Shh." He cocked his head. "They're over there. No." He pointed. "Over there—"

"Court, wake up." Rebecca reached for his hand.

Blindly he pushed her away. "They're all around us. Ben. Ben," he whispered. "Jamie's been hit. Ben. Talk to me. Oh, no. Jamie. Where's Jamie?"

Rebecca watched helplessly. She didn't know what to do.

Somewhere she'd read not to awaken someone having a nightmare. But to watch this was unbearable.

Now tears were streaming down his cheeks. He reached out, stroking his phantom comrade. "Oh, Jamie. Jamie."

"Court—"

He grabbed her wrist pulling her to him. "Fire. We'll be burned alive. We've got to get out of here." With his other hand he shielded his face. "Do you smell it, the fire? Do you smell the flesh burning? Blood. Oh, God, the blood. Help us. Oh, dear God, help us. Help us. . . ."

Rebecca pulled free. "Court! Court, you're having a nightmare. Wake up."

"Too late." He buried his face in his hands. "Too late, too late," he repeated in despair. "Too late. They're dead. They're all dead," he sobbed.

Rebecca dropped down onto the couch beside him.

She wrapped her arms around him and held him close. She held him as she would a wounded child, his head against her heart, rocking him in her arms while she murmured words of comfort.

How long she remained, she couldn't guess. She stayed until her arms ached and grew numb. And even then, when she gently disengaged, she didn't leave him but curled up in the great leather chair and dozed until the first finger of dawn poked between the drapes.

Court woke to find her there.

His face was haggard, not just from fatigue, but from humiliation. She could see it in his eyes.

"So now you know," he said.

"I already knew—"

"Jack told you."

"He didn't go into detail. He just told me what had happened and how brave you were."

"That's a laugh." Court's voice was bitter.

Rebecca knelt next to him. She took his hands in both of hers and looked up into his eyes, demanding his attention. "You were brave," she said, with ferocious certainty. "Everyone knows that. . .but you."

He turned away. "So brave that every night my failure and my fear come back to haunt me? If I can't die, dear God"— he raised his eyes heavenward—"at least let me sleep."

Rebecca lifted her hand and stroked his cheek. She wanted to say something to comfort him, but he was beyond comfort, drowning in his own torment and guilt.

"I barely close my eyes, and it starts all over again, that last battle with all the shouting and horror. And the smells. The smells—jungle smells and the stench of burning flesh. And the blood, everywhere blood. Even the rain couldn't wash away all that blood." He closed his eyes as if he were willing himself to suffer the atrocities one more time. His penance.

If only she could offer him the solace of those words from the Psalms that had given such comfort to her when she'd lost David. *God is our refuge and strength, a very present help in trouble. Therefore will not we fear, though the earth be removed, and though the mountains be carried into the midst of the sea.*

She'd been lucky. She'd had the love and support of her family. More important, she'd kept what Court had lost. Her faith.

His fists clenched. "Even the headaches are better than this." He was sheathed in sweat, the afghan she'd thrown over him bunched at his feet.

She urged him to lie back, to close his eyes. She stroked his brow, his clenched fists until they loosened and lay inert by his sides. Weary, she rested her head against his shoulder.

"Mommy." Davy stood at the end of the couch, rubbing his eyes. "I didn't know where you were."

"Davy, you woke up early." She jumped to her feet and hurried to him. "I'm sorry, Darling. I hope you weren't scared. You know Mommy's always nearby."

"I was scared at first. But I remembered what you say."

She gave him a hug. "What smart thing was that?"

"You say, if I get scared, remember God is with me, even if I don't see Him."

Out of the mouths of babes. . . .

He trotted around the end of the couch. "What's wrong with Mr. Court?"

"He's not feeling well, Dear," Rebecca said, turning Davy around and urging him toward the door. But he pulled from her grasp and ran back.

He threw his arms around Court's neck. "I'm sorry you're sick, Mr. Court. Where does it hurt?"

Rebecca was about to pull him away when the expression on Court's face stopped her. It was so profoundly sad as he gazed into her son's earnest brown eyes. He put his arm around Davy and held him close. "It hurts here, Davy," he said, laying his hand over his heart.

❧

For the next few days Rebecca tried to carry on as before, but it wasn't the same. It never would be. She'd had a painful glimpse into Court's soul. She doubted he could ever forgive her for that.

Davy, she, and Court continued to take their meals together, but Court never lingered. Following dinner he'd sequester himself in the library as he'd done in the beginning. But now, making sure the door was securely closed.

It was mid-afternoon, a week later. Davy was napping, and Rebecca was curled up on the couch in the solarium reading when Court wheeled into the room. "I was wondering if the mail had arrived."

"Not yet."

She was surprised when he rolled closer. He had not been inclined to sociability of late.

"What's that you're reading?"

"An article."

"Oh?" He waited. When no further information was forthcoming, he said, "What's it about? Is it something I'd be interested in?"

Rebecca was not at all anxious to share it with him. "Oh, it's just—sort of a layman's, ah—"

"Sounds fascinating. Now you've really piqued my curiosity," he said dryly.

She gave him a long, thoughtful look and decided to tell him. "It's an article on hysterical paralysis."

Court's blue eyes chilled. The muscle in his jaw twitched. "Working on your thesis, Dr. Spaneas?" he growled. "You've certainly acquired plenty of anecdotal material."

"That's not fair." She uncurled her legs and set her feet firmly on the floor. Looking him directly in the eye, she said, "We care about you—"

"We?"

"Davy and I."

"Oh, I see," he growled again. "He's working on his doctorate, too."

"All right, I care then. I want to understand—"

"Why are you bothering? You're only going to be here a few more weeks."

"That doesn't mean we'll never see each other again. We can still be friends."

Court sighed. "Why would you want to be my friend? I've given you nothing but trouble since the day you arrived."

She gave him a wry smile. "Well, you have done that. But now and then I see a little compensating spark that suggests maybe there's some hope for your redemption."

He looked at her thoughtfully then finally settled back into his wheelchair and folded his arms. "So what new insight do you have to tell me that I don't already know?"

"Probably nothing. But it's interesting to me. You're sure you want to hear it?"

"No, but go ahead anyway."

Rebecca looked down at the paper she was holding. "Of course it starts with a definition: Hysterical paralysis is conversion of emotional stress or mental disturbance into a physical symptom. . . For example, blindness, inability to speak"—she glanced up—"paralysis, or another sudden debilitating problem for no reason evident through testing."

"Sounds like something my psychiatrist might have written."

Rebecca continued. "Then it goes on about anxiety and depression—" She flipped through the sheets. "I thought this was interesting. Acute battle-incurred neurosis. . . ." She ran her finger down the page. "Here it is." She cleared her throat. "Guilt centering about an inability to remain in combat after a long period of good service. An example. . .his men killed, couldn't sleep, irritability, obsessive thought about lost men, amnesia—"

She glanced up then back at the sheet. "It says here that it often happens to men who were previously well adjusted with high personal expectations." She flipped the page. "Men with acute battle-incurred neurosis are sometimes less responsive to psychotherapy. In other words—"

"That's enough, Rebecca," he said harshly. "I'm well aware of the symptoms."

"You're right. I'm sorry. But just listen to one more thing.

Here are the stages of recovery."

"I've heard enough." Court's hands went toward the push rim of his chair, but she grabbed his wrist.

"You've got to listen to this part. It's the most important."

"I don't got to do anything."

He tried to shake her off, but she wouldn't let go.

"This is where we can be part of your therapy."

"We?"

"Those of us who love you."

He looked at her curiously. "Do you know what you just said?"

She thought. "I said, those of us who—you know what I mean."

"What do you mean?"

"You know. In the—in the generic sense." That her feelings for Courtney Fielding were anything more than attraction, profound though that might be, was not an admission she was ready to make to herself, let alone him.

"Well. You got my attention."

"Are you going to listen? Or do I have to keep holding on to you?"

"If I have a choice—"

"No, you don't." She released him and thumbed through to the last page of the article. "Here it is. It says here that 'the most important first step in recovery is having the courage to reconstruct and mourn the traumatic loss. Even though one is responsible for his own recovery, it must take place in the context of relationships and depends on the discovery of restorative love—'"

"In the generic sense," he said it with indifference, but his eyes sent quite the opposite message.

"And finally," she said, "reconnection, the task of creating a future, depends on developing a sustaining faith."

His gaze was long and steady.

Rebecca didn't flinch.

After what seemed endless minutes, he reached out his hand. "May I read that article, please?"

twenty-one

It was mid-afternoon, late September, hot and sticky. Court could hear Manuel's mower around the side of the house as he sat on the patio watching Davy and Rebecca play tag on the lawn. She wore blue shorts and a white cotton shirt. Her dark hair hung free, whipping around her shoulders as she ran, racing and reaching for her child with the joy and enthusiasm of a child herself.

Long-limbed and lithe, she took his breath away.

As he watched, Court remembered that night in the library, two weeks ago, when she'd witnessed his nightmare. He would never forget the feel of her cool hand on his brow or the soothing comfort of her voice or the refuge he took in her chaste embrace.

It had been an epiphany for him. The worst had been exposed. He no longer needed to hide. The moment of healing had begun.

How arrogant he'd been to think God would single him out for suffering. He had been blaming God for man's transgressions. Sadly he'd come to realize that men of good intention could come into the crossfire of evil men's crimes.

Despite that price, Rebecca had reminded him about the wisdom of God's gift of free will. For with free will also came the opportunity to experience the joy of spiritual and personal growth and accomplishment. Gifts that made worldly possessions seem paltry by comparison. They were unique. They could not be stolen. But they could be shared.

With her encouragement he had begun to paint again.

But this process of reconciliation was slow and painful. He had come to realize that he could never expect complete resolution. He would always remember, but as time went on, he would learn to cope with the memories. He struggled to come to terms with the past as he began to reclaim the present.

"Hey, Mr. Court. Look what I can do." Davy executed a lopsided somersault.

"Good job, Davy."

Rebecca grinned, clapping.

Rebecca and Davy were part of this new present. Perhaps not in the way he dreamed. That, too, defied resolution. He loved her. Simply. Completely. With his whole heart. He loved her enough to be willing to be just her friend. He had reconciled himself to that.

Davy ran up the patio steps. Breathless, he leaned against Court's legs. "Can we draw after dinner tonight, Mr. Court?"

Court patted his arm. "Sure can, Davy."

"Good!" Davy was off. Racing down the steps, he jumped into his mother's arms, and they rolled, giggling, onto the lawn.

Rebecca untangled herself and stood up, dusting the grass from her shorts. She waved at Court.

He waved back, then realized she wasn't waving at him. He swung his chair around to see Jack striding across the patio toward him.

As far as Court was concerned, Jack had been making a nuisance of himself lately—usually at dinnertime. Court couldn't blame him. After all, he was a bachelor, and Rebecca turned out the best meal in town. But Court's days with her were numbered and too precious to share, even with his best friend. Especially when it was quite clear that his best friend had developed an interest that went beyond the food she served.

Let him enjoy her on his own time, after Rebecca and Davy had moved in with Miss Bufford and Court didn't have to witness it.

"Hi, old man." Jack cuffed him on the shoulder.

"Hello. You here to dinner?" *Again?*

"Unfortunately I'm headed to a potluck at the church."

Court breathed an inner sigh of relief. "I remember those dinners. An abundance of carrot and raisin salad, ambrosia—with extra marshmallows and coconut—and tuna casserole with bread crumbs on top."

Jack laughed. "You got it, Man. Why don't you join us?"

"Are you kidding? When I can eat Rebecca's food?"

"Bring her and Davy. They might welcome a night out."

"I think I could find a more attractive spot for a night out than your church fellowship hall." He grinned. "Maybe next time."

"Which brings me to why I'm here," Jack said. "Do you have time to talk?"

"Sure. Pull up one of those lounge chairs."

"In private."

"This sounds like serious business."

"It is. About as serious as it gets."

Rebecca called, "Are you staying to dinner, Jack?"

"Yes. Stay! Stay! Stay!" Davy chorused, bounding up the steps. He ran over and threw his arms around Jack's knees.

Jack leaned down and gave him a hug. "Can I have a rain check?" he called to Rebecca.

"Sure. But you better turn it in quick. I'll be moving in two weeks, you know."

Court's stomach tightened. He'd tried not to think about that and wasn't happy to be reminded.

Jack followed him back across the patio and into the library. Instead of dropping onto the couch with his usual abandon, he commenced pacing.

Court parked behind the desk. "So what's up?"

Jack stopped abruptly, frowned, chewed on his lower lip and shoved his hands into his pockets. He took a deep breath. "I'm going to ask Rebecca to marry me."

Court felt as if he'd been hit in the chest with a mace. He could hardly breathe.

He'd seen the signs, so why was he so surprised? Why did he feel so betrayed? An irrational mix of anger at his friend, hopelessness, and despair exploded within him. No matter the logic in his head, his heart had nurtured hope.

"Well? What do you think?" Jack asked.

"You're sure it's not just her cooking?" Court managed.

"Are you kidding? Yeah, you're kidding." Jack grinned nervously and got a blissful expression on his face. "Cooking is the least of her talents. She's a great mother. She's patient and compassionate."

Court didn't need a litany of Rebecca's wonderful qualities. He was an expert on them.

Jack continued. "And she's tactful. Which is very important in a minister's wife. She'll be able to cope with the congregation. In fact, they already love her."

"It sounds as if you've given it a lot of thought."

"Believe me, I have."

"So what does it matter what I think?" Court said quietly. "You love her. That's what's important."

Jack's declaration had made Court realize that, despite claiming to have no illusions about Rebecca, he'd had plenty. He'd just refused to admit them.

"The problem is," Jack was saying, "I'm her minister. That's a unique and important relationship in a person's life. I don't want to jeopardize that if she doesn't have the same feelings for me that I have for her."

Court wanted to hate him. It would be so much easier if he had a target, someone to blame. But there was no blame.

Looking up into his friend's decent, honest face, he could only believe that the woman who chose Jack McCutcheon for a husband would get the best. And the best was what Rebecca deserved.

"Go for it," Court said. "She can't say yes if you don't ask the question." He smiled into his friend's eyes. "If it's meant to be, it will be."

"You sound almost biblical." Jack smiled. "How about instead, 'The will of the Lord be done?'"

Court forced himself to return his friend's smile. Perhaps if there was any consolation, it was that he, Court, was part of God's plan for Rebecca's happiness. After all, if she hadn't come to be his housekeeper, she would never have met Jack. He shook his head. "If you weren't such a great guy—"

"Let's hope Rebecca thinks so."

"She'd be a fool not to," Court said quietly. "And Rebecca's no fool."

❧

Two nights later Jack took Rebecca to dinner.

"Not in the fellowship hall, I trust," Court had said.

"You trust right." Jack had grinned.

"And I suppose you want me to baby-sit."

"If you wouldn't mind."

"Sure. I'll be glad to." Court almost expected his nose to grow with that lie.

Now, with Davy tucked safely in bed, he was in the library, finishing some paperwork at his desk, trying not to think of what was taking place. He glanced at the clock. She'd been gone two hours.

"You knew, didn't you." It wasn't a question. Rebecca stood in the door, leaning against the jamb.

She was wearing a simple black sheath that skimmed her slender body, its only embellishment a string of pearls. With her thick hair pulled back from her face, her dark eyes looked enormous. To Court, she was breathtakingly beautiful.

"You knew he was going to propose."

Court nodded. This was a conversation he'd wanted to avoid. He'd hoped by the time she came home, he'd be in bed. But she'd returned early. What kind of a sign was that?

"Are you interested in my answer?" she asked.

"Of course."

"I told him I was honored, and I'd think about it." She floated across the room on a cloud of lilac perfume and dropped into the chair across the desk from him.

It was more than a man should have to bear.

"Oh, Court, I'm fond of him, deeply fond of him. But I still can only think of him as 'Pastor Jack.' He's such an honorable, fine man, and I know he'd make a good father for Davy. It's just that my marriage was so perfect before. I'm afraid—"

"Only God is perfect," Court said dryly.

"That's amusing, coming from you."

"Face it, Rebecca. You weren't married long enough for you to see his imperfections. Death does tend to sanitize one's character, you know."

Rebecca's eyes flashed. "What's your point? Are you implying—"

"—that he wasn't a saint? Don't make his shoes too big to fill, Rebecca. It's not fair to the next man you marry. And certainly not fair to expect of a four-year-old child. It's time Davy had a human father to look up to, and there could be none better than Jack McCutcheon."

"You have your nerve." Rebecca stood up and looked down at him disdainfully. "What makes you such an expert in child rearing and matrimony? David Spaneas may or may not have been a saint, but he lived by God's laws, and for as long as he inhabited this earth, he tried to fulfill God's purpose for his life. Even saints can't do better than that. I'm proud I was his wife. And I'm proud that I can hold him up as an example to our son."

The sight of her, flushed, burning with passion and anger ignited a responding fire in Court. If the desk hadn't been between them, he doubted he could have resisted the temptation to reach out to her, pull her down into his arms, and hold her as he'd yearned to do since the first moment he'd set eyes on her.

She took a gulp of air. "Unlike some people who have squandered their God-given intelligence and talent." She looked Court in the eye. "Have you ever for a moment considered that *you* might have been an example of faith and courage to some child? I doubt it."

Court stared back at her, frowning. "Did I miss something? You didn't come in here to talk about me. You came in to talk about Jack."

"Well, that's lucky," she said, turning on her heel. "Because you are the last man on earth I would ever consider marrying."

He watched her stride out the door. "I didn't ask you to," he murmured.

twenty-two

Near tears, Rebecca stamped up the stairs.

How dare he, deprecating her dead husband, telling her how she should raise her son, foisting her off on his best friend. Court's words stuck in her brain and stuck in her craw.

She yanked open the door to her quarters then remembered Davy asleep in the bedroom and closed it quietly behind her.

First thing she'd done when she'd left Jack was to run into the library and confide in Court.

Why? What had she hoped to accomplish?

Certainly not what she got.

She tiptoed into Davy's room. The nightlight cast a warm comforting glow over the scattered toys. Court was not the tough taskmaster she was when it came to her son's tidiness.

Extricating George from the tangled sheets, she tucked him back into Davy's arms and secured the covers around them both. She leaned over and dropped a kiss on her son's soft cheek. Gazing down at her blessed boy, she reflected on Court's words.

How could he criticize her? It was her duty as a mother to provide a strong male image for her son. What better example than his own father? she thought belligerently. And yet perfection was an impossible path to follow. Was she really pressing that burden on Davy?

In the sitting room where she slept, Rebecca removed her clothes and put on her nightgown. She stacked the throw pillows on the adjacent chair, neatly folded back the slipcover on the daybed and slid under the covers.

She closed her eyes and commenced with a cursory

version of her nightly prayers, which were now continually interrupted by rebellious thoughts of her confrontation with Court.

Amen! She flopped over onto her stomach.

She turned on her side, adjusted the pillow, pushed down the blanket, pulled it up. Closed the window. When the room got stuffy, she got up and opened it.

It was hopeless!

This wasn't the first time Courtney Fielding had kept her awake. For one reason or another he'd been doing it since the day she'd arrived.

But, recently, the reasons had improved immeasurably. They had developed an empathy for each other, an understanding. And certainly he had bonded with Davy. She'd learned to deal with his artistic temperament and volatility, to count on his gentle concern and admire his unpredictable humor and his intelligence.

But, finally, she'd had to admit, it wasn't just his mind to which she was attracted.

Why else would she allow herself to be buffeted about by his whims? Why else was she enamored with the look in his eyes or the brief touch of his hand?

Surely there was something in the Bible that warned against such weakness.

The words of First Corinthians chapter ten, verse thirteen, popped into her head. The ones her mother had her commit to memory when she turned sixteen and was invited to the senior prom. *There hath no temptation taken you but such as is common to man: but God is faithful, who will not suffer you to be tempted above that ye are able—* She couldn't remember the rest, but that would do.

Not that Court had shown impropriety. Far from it. Her own imagination, her own willful need, brought on temptation.

Yet she'd glimpsed desire in his eyes, too. Even tonight as he'd urged her to accept his friend's proposal. His own need. His own passion.

She was sure of it.

Get hold of yourself, Girl! Too much was at stake to allow the weakness of the flesh to overcome the calling of the spirit.

Get back to what was important!

First and foremost, she had Davy's welfare to consider. She must focus on that. *Be patient and listen for God's direction.*

Had God offered direction through Court's words? Rebecca sat up and stared out the window into the night.

Setting aside the rancor, the embarrassment, she began to see that Court was right about Davy. Even about Jack. The Lord did work in mysterious ways. Once again he'd set her up to hear the truth. She sighed. But it could have been said nicer.

She slid out of bed and pulled on her robe. Quietly she opened the door and padded down the back stairs in her bare feet. As she often did when she couldn't sleep, she warmed some milk then carried the cup into the solarium.

Tonight there was a full moon, and the room was bathed in silver, like some mystical place in a far-off fantasy.

"You couldn't sleep either?"

Rebecca almost dropped her cup. "Court?"

"Who were you expecting? The boogie-man?" The light next to the couch went on. "Well, here I am."

It took a moment for her eyes to adjust, an awkward moment when she was trying to figure out what to say.

Court saved her the trouble. "About tonight, I had no right to—"

"But you did. I gave you the right when I came into the library and confided in you."

"No, I wasn't fair. You're a terrific mother."

"I won't dispute that." Rebecca laughed softly. "But I've been thinking about what you said. I needed to hear it.

Davy's little now, and it hasn't affected him, but as he gets older, setting up a saint to live up to is an impossible goal for a child. . .and a husband."

"Please, Rebecca. This isn't necessary."

"No, let me finish." She put her cup down on the coffee table and walked over to him. "You were right about Jack, too. Without question he is one of the finest, most compassionate, most honorable, most loving men—people—I have ever known. I admire him with all my heart, and he would make a wonderful father for Davy—"

"You've made the right decision."

"But I don't love him."

Court looked at her as if he hadn't understood.

Quietly she said, "Not in the way a woman should love the man she marries." She held Court's gaze without moving. She couldn't have moved if she'd wanted to.

A protracted silence fell between them.

She saw the confusion, the turmoil—the relief in his expressive blue eyes.

Couldn't he likewise see her feelings for him? Her love?

She'd said as much as she dared. Now it was up to him.

&

Court cleared his throat.

Was he hearing her correctly? Was he seeing in her eyes what he had dreamed of seeing?

She surely knew him. The good and the bad. Was it possible that this beautiful, dynamic, spiritual woman could love an irascible sinner like him? Enough to marry him?

That alone could restore a man's faith.

"I have something for you," he said.

He could see the disappointment in Rebecca's eyes.

Clearly she had expected—hoped—for more from him. A declaration of affection at the very least.

All in good time.

He wheeled around and motioned her to follow him. In the library he flicked on the desk lamp. He picked up a beige envelope and handed it to her.

"It's addressed to you," she said.

"Read it."

She pulled two sheets from the envelope. Her mouth dropped open as she read. "Oh, Court, I can't believe it. They want to see a synopsis and the first three chapters of *The Amazing Davy and His Time Machine*." She looked up. "How did it happen?"

Court looked smug. "Remember those notes you gave me? Well, I drafted a query letter to my editor. That's what I got back."

"Well," she said half seriously, "I'd only consider it if you did the illustrations."

"Read on."

She turned the page and laughed. "*They'll* only consider it if you do the illustrations."

He grinned. "What do you say? Shall we form a collaboration?"

"What do you think I say? Of course." She leaned over and threw her arms around his neck. "Oh, Court, you've given me so much."

"A lot of heartache, I'm afraid," he said. "You might want to reconsider when you know the extenuating circumstances."

"I can't imagine."

"What if I told you I'd fallen hopelessly, helplessly in love with you? That I can't imagine life without you."

"And Davy?" Her smile was sweet with the confidence of his answer.

"Especially Davy."

Her eyes were dreamy and diffused. "Even that wouldn't make me change my mind," she murmured, sliding into his lap. "Oh, Court, I love you, too. I love you so much. Why do you think I couldn't say yes to Jack?"

He wrapped his arms around her, breathing in the lingering scent of her perfume; he combed his fingers through the thick, silken strands of her dark hair. With every beat of his heart, with every breath that he drew, he loved her.

Silently, before God, he vowed that even if he never walked again, he would be a man of courage and faith. A man who didn't need the use of his legs to make him whole. A man worthy of Rebecca's love and devotion.

He pulled her close and did what he'd wanted to do since the moment she'd walked into his life. He kissed her slow and sweet with a languid passion. As if he had all the time in the world.

epilogue

It was a simple afternoon ceremony in early January, in the little church in Eagle Rock. Jack officiated, blessing the union of Rebecca and Court despite his own deep disappointment. As a surprise Court had flown Rebecca's father from the Philippines to give the bride away.

Rebecca had arranged the two fluted wedding baskets flanking the dais with branches of white camellias that Manuel, the caretaker and gardener, had gathered from the Fielding estate.

Only a few close friends and family clustered in the pews at the front of the little sanctuary. Miss Bufford was among them, assisted by a retired nurse who had taken what was to be Rebecca's place—much more suitable for the position.

Precious Ada, the flowers on her new hat aquiver, sat in the front row on the groom's side, between her grandson, Paul, and Manuel. Across the aisle was Rebecca's father's second wife, Goldie. No replacement for Rebecca's dear, departed mother, but a worthy and beloved partner and loving stepmother.

In a blue silk dress the color of forget-me-nots, wearing a crown of sweet-scented plumeria, lilies-of-the-valley, and baby's breath, Rebecca waited in the narthex, her arm linked through her father's. She held the small white Bible that had once belonged to her mother.

"Now, Mommy? Now?" Davy clutched the satin pillow bearing the double rings, George (bathed for the occasion) tucked under his arm. He shifted nervously from one foot to the other.

"You don't have to go to the rest room, do you, Honey?" Rebecca asked anxiously.

"No, I'm just excited. When do I get to give Daddy Court the rings?"

"It won't be long now, Mister Davy," Rebecca's father assured him.

Rebecca caught Daisy's eye and smiled.

Dear Daisy, whose friend and confidante she had become, her maid of honor. Daisy who had started it all. How could anyone resist the blonde, curly-haired Daisy? The will-o-the-wisp, a breath of spring, who spread joy and sunshine wherever she walked. Rebecca prayed that Jack would recognize the woman in the girl who had always loved him.

As strains of the traditional wedding song "Oh, Promise Me" floated through the little church, Rebecca thought of her sister, Imogene, and husband Jimmy, missionaries in Japan. Once again Imogene was missing Rebecca's wedding. The first time the war had interfered; this time the blessed arrival of a precious new baby girl.

Finally the wedding march began.

Daisy disappeared into the sanctuary, Davy at her side.

Rebecca looked up into the weathered face of her treasured father. His eyes were suspiciously bright as he leaned down and kissed her cheek. "It's our turn now, Becky, girl."

Rebecca nodded, too moved to speak.

As she and her father passed through the double doors and down the center aisle Rebecca met the gaze of her beloved Court waiting next to his boyhood friend, Jack.

The only wedding gift Rebecca had prayed for, she'd received. With the supportive prayers of those who loved him and months of arduous therapy—physical, mental, and spiritual—Court walked again.

Now he stood, unaided, strong and tall, healed by God's grace and the power of His restorative love.

A Letter To Our Readers

Dear Reader:

In order that we might better contribute to your reading enjoyment, we would appreciate your taking a few minutes to respond to the following questions. We welcome your comments and read each form and letter we receive. When completed, please return to the following:

Fiction Editor
Heartsong Presents
PO Box 719
Uhrichsville, Ohio 44683

1. Did you enjoy reading *The Healing Heart* by Rachel Druten?
   ❑ Very much! I would like to see more books by this author!
   ❑ Moderately. I would have enjoyed it more if

   _____

   _____

   _____

2. Are you a member of **Heartsong Presents**?   ❑ Yes   ❑ No
   If no, where did you purchase this book?_____

   _____

3. How would you rate, on a scale from 1 (poor) to 5 (superior),
   the cover design? _____

4. On a scale from 1 (poor) to 10 (superior), please rate the
   following elements.

   ____ Heroine   ____ Plot
   ____ Hero   ____ Inspirational theme
   ____ Setting   ____ Secondary characters

5. These characters were special because?_____
   _____
   _____

6. How has this book inspired your life?_____
   _____
   _____

7. What settings would you like to see covered in future
   Heartsong Presents books? _____
   _____
   _____

8. What are some inspirational themes you would like to see
   treated in future books? _____
   _____
   _____

9. Would you be interested in reading other **Heartsong
   Presents** titles? ☐ Yes ☐ No

10. Please check your age range:
    ☐ Under 18   ☐ 18-24
    ☐ 25-34   ☐ 35-45
    ☐ 46-55   ☐ Over 55

Name_____
Occupation _____
Address _____
City_____ State_____ Zip_____

TUCSON

Travel back in time to the 1870s when a small fort protected settlers of the Arizona desert—and a small town called Tucson was beginning to flourish. Meet the women who made faith, hope, and love blossom under the blazing sun.

Follow the fascinating life journeys of four pioneering women. Can they learn to love the land, its Creator, and the men who tame the wild desert?

Historical, paperback, 480 pages, 5 ³/₁₆" x 8"

❤ ❤ ❤ ❤ ❤ ❤ ❤ ❤ ❤ ❤ ❤ ❤ ❤ ❤ ❤

Please send me _____ copies of *Tucson*. I am enclosing $6.99 for each. (Please add $2.00 to cover postage and handling per order. OH add 7% tax.)

Send check or money order, no cash or C.O.D.s please.

Name _____

Address _____

City, State, Zip _____

To place a credit card order, call 1-800-847-8270.
Send to: Heartsong Presents Reader Service, PO Box 721, Uhrichsville, OH 44683

❤ ❤ ❤ ❤ ❤ ❤ ❤ ❤ ❤ ❤ ❤ ❤ ❤ ❤ ❤

Heart song

$\mathcal{H}$EARTSONG ♥ PRESENTS

Love Stories
Are Rated G!

That's for godly, gratifying, and of course, great! If you love a thrilling love story but don't appreciate the sordidness of some popular paperback romances, **Heartsong Presents** is for you. In fact, **Heartsong Presents** is the premiere inspirational romance book club featuring love stories where Christian faith is the primary ingredient in a marriage relationship.

Sign up today to receive your first set of four, never-before-published Christian romances. Send no money now; you will receive a bill with the first shipment. You may cancel at any time without obligation, and if you aren't completely satisfied with any selection, you may return the books for an immediate refund!

Imagine. . .four new romances every four weeks—two historical, two contemporary—with men and women like you who long to meet the one God has chosen as the love of their lives. . .all for the low price of $10.99 postpaid.

To join, simply complete the coupon below and mail to the address provided. **Heartsong Presents** romances are rated G for another reason: They'll arrive Godspeed!

YES! Sign me up for Heart♥ng!

NEW MEMBERSHIPS WILL BE SHIPPED IMMEDIATELY!
Send no money now. We'll bill you only $10.99 post-paid with your first shipment of four books. Or for faster action, call toll free 1-800-847-8270.

NAME _____

ADDRESS _____

CITY _____STATE _____ ZIP_____

MAIL TO: HEARTSONG PRESENTS, P.O. Box 721, Uhrichsville, Ohio 44683
or visit www.heartsongpresents.com